40 DAYS IN
HICKSVILLE

40 DAYS IN
HICKSVILLE

Christina Kilbourne

We acknowledge financial support for our publishing activities: the
Government of Canada, through the Canada Book Fund and The Canada Council
for the Arts; the Government of Ontario, through the Ontario Arts Council, Ontario
Creates, and the Ontario Book Publishing Tax Credit. We acknowledge additional
funding provided by the Government of Ontario and the Ontario Arts Council to
address the adverse effects of the novel coronavirus pandemic.

Library and Archives Canada Cataloguing in Publication

Title: 40 days in Hicksville / Christina Kilbourne.
Other titles: Forty days in Hicksville
Names: Kilbourne, Christina, author.
Identifiers: Canadiana (print) 20230207162 | Canadiana (ebook) 20230207170 |
ISBN 9781770867154 (softcover) | ISBN 9781770867161 (HTML)
Classification: LCC PS8571.I476 A6125 2023 | DDC jC813/.6—dc23

United States Library of Congress Control Number: 2023934879

Cover images: iStock
Cover design: Marijke Friesen
Interior text design: Marijke Friesen
Manufactured by Friesens in Altona, Manitoba in July, 2023.

MIX
Paper from
responsible sources
FSC® C016245

Printed using paper from a responsible and sustainable resource,
including a mix of virgin fibres and recycled materials.

Printed and bound in Canada.

DCB Young Readers
An imprint of Cormorant Books Inc.
260 Ishpadinaa (Spadina) Avenue, Suite 502, Tkaronto (Toronto), ON M5T 2E4
www.dcbyoungreaders.com
www.cormorantbooks.com

In Memory of John Patrick McCormick Jr.
and Lloyd Eric Larsfolk

ZACH 1

Mrs. Purvis is in the middle of a lesson on common rebel archetypes in contemporary literature when the classroom door opens and the principal walks in. A step behind is this girl with wild blond hair and an even wilder attitude.

She's wearing ripped jeans and an ink-blue sweater, the slouchy kind that reminds me of pictures of my mom in the eighties. She's wearing a worn-in pair of Blundstones and an expression that says *I'm so supremely pissed* and *eff-you* and *just try me* all at the same time. When she turns her head, I can see that, although her hair is long, the back of her neck is shaved up to the base of her skull. I mean, who does that?

The principal smiles at Mrs. P. "This is Kate Cooper. She just moved here from out west."

Mrs. P smiles back. "Welcome, Kate. Why don't you take the empty seat beside Sydney?" She motions toward the back of the room, and Sydney chews her thumbnail as Kate walks toward her. The principal leaves, and Mrs. P continues her lesson. "We were discussing the characteristics of rebels, Kate. Perhaps there's a rebellious character in a book or movie that you admire and can tell us why?"

Kate slumps into the empty desk without saying a word and Mrs. P doesn't miss a beat. "Sydney was telling us that she admires the noble rebel because this character has a purpose and leads a worthy cause, like Nelson Mandela or Martin Luther King Jr."

Kate throws a sideways glance at Sydney, who starts chewing on her other thumbnail in response. Somehow I doubt they're going to strike up an everlasting friendship.

Nobody is looking at Mrs. P, and they probably aren't listening either. Instead, everybody is staring at the new girl, me included. Like, nobody is even shy about staring. If we were apes, we'd probably be hooting and jumping around to get her attention. You can tell from a half-second glance that this girl is never going to fit in at our school. I mean, she's so sophisticated she seems like a whole new species. Like, again, if we're all apes, she's a panther.

But Mrs. P doesn't let our collective inattention put her off her game. She goes on to explain the differences between the anarchist rebel, the social rebel, and the feminist rebel and notes that the unique challenge facing the rebel archetype is discovering creative, productive ways to utilize their rebellious nature without allowing it to become destructive.

"Does this make sense to you, Kate?"

Again, Kate doesn't answer, but stares at Mrs. P with lowered lids, resentment boiling just below the surface.

I shift my gaze between Kate and Mrs. P, wondering why Mrs. P is coming down so hard on her. I mean, Kate hasn't even taken out a notebook or pen, she's barely had a chance to warm her seat.

Finally, Kate speaks. "I guess. Whatever."

Mrs. P assesses Kate as if she's trying to decide what number Kate should get on the pain-in-the-ass scale.

"Do you appreciate the role of rebels in today's music?"

The question is a trap and I want to save Kate from answering it wrong. I want to run to her side and whisk her away, out through the classroom door and into one of my dad's old Indiana Jones movies. But before I can even flinch, or fully return from my fantasy, Kate mutters.

"Not really. Rebels are overrated bullshit."

From where I'm sitting, I can see Kate holding her phone under the desk, angling it up toward Mrs. P's face. There's a small red light blinking and my jaw drops. Is she taking a video? I glance at my friend Josh to see if he's seeing what I'm seeing and from the look on his face, I can tell he hasn't missed a thing.

"What makes you say that?" Mrs. P asks, unaware she's being filmed.

I'm sure by now, Kate wishes she'd never opened her mouth because Mrs. P, like any good teacher, is about to *involve* Kate and that defeats the whole point of Kate's reluctance in the first place. Kate continues to film the conversation.

Mrs. P turns to the class. "Who agrees with Kate? Are rebels overrated bullshit?"

The noise level in the room goes off the decibel chart when Mrs. P says *bullshit*. Kate's shoulders straighten in surprise. I guess they don't condone teacher profanity in classrooms where she's from.

As for me, I'm no longer paying attention to Mrs. P's lesson. I can't take my eyes off Kate. She's tucked her phone in her back pocket and is gripping her backpack like she's on the verge of bolting. Everyone else is watching her too, like she holds a classified secret from the future that they need to know. Then Kate looks up and catches me staring at her. Our eyes lock and she snarls. I look away and don't dare sneak a look for the rest of class.

But by then it's too late. I can feel her across the room. Kate Cooper has been in my world for less than an hour and I already know she's someone I want to know more about. *Really*. I mean, I would have mocked such a declaration last week if it was written in a novel, all that crap about chemistry. But maybe it really happens.

Needless to say, I try to find Kate at lunch. But not in an obvious way. Instead of staring at the floor like I normally do when I walk to my locker, I keep my head upright. She isn't in the hall or the cafeteria so I lap the courtyard. Still nothing. Finally, I see her outside, coming from the direction of downtown. She's alone and still wearing her backpack like she hasn't bothered to get a locker and isn't planning on returning Monday morning.

✗ ✗ ✗

After lunch I go to anthro, but Kate isn't there. In fact, I don't see her until after school when I climb on the bus. I look toward the back seat where Josh is sitting and there she is! She's on my bus! Who says there's no God? She's sitting by herself next to the window and I want to slide in beside her, but something inside me yells: *Not cool! Not cool! Retreat!*

I sit behind her instead. And try to act disinterested in everything around me.

"Hey! Zach! There's room back here, remember?" Josh shouts. I wave to silence him and jerk my head toward Kate. He rolls his eyes and grins like: *Good luck with that.*

Josh and I have been friends since grade five when we both realized we didn't have a competitive advantage on the sports field, which is all that matters when it comes to social hierarchy at that age. He was small for his age and I couldn't score a goal if the soccer net was the size of the school. So we sat on the sidelines together and talked about Rick Riordan novels and Greek mythology until grade eight when he finally hit his growth spurt. I still have lousy coordination, but he's still my best friend.

When the bus stops at Josh's house, he bumps my shoulder on his way past and mutters, "Bros before hoes," which is not as offensive as it sounds. It's an inside joke from this time we were at the plowing match. Anyway, it's a long story. The point is, I know he's not mad at me for sitting at the front near Kate.

The bus turns onto Valley Road and Kate is still on the bus. She's listening to music through her earphones and videoing the farms sliding by the bus window. Although she's playing her music so loud I can make out the words, I don't recognize any of the songs. It sounds pretty intense. Like heavy metal on speed.

"Anytime today, Zach," the bus driver yells.

We're stopped at my driveway and the door is wide open, but my brain is still processing the music. I stumble by and try to catch her attention, but she just stares at her backpack. I think I see tears pooling at the edge of her eyes, but I walk past too quickly to be sure. Outside I stand on the side of the road as the bus pulls away. It takes a few minutes before I can convince my legs to move. On the way by, I stop at the mailbox. We have one of those tacky ones shaped like a fish. I reach inside. Among the bills there's a postcard for me. From Mom. From Mongolia. Although I know from Facebook she's already in Nepal. I sniff it instinctively but there's no trace of her smell. As usual she signed

Love, Mom but nothing about *wish you were here*. And nothing about missing Dad or asking how he's doing, like he's been erased.

Just seeing her handwriting makes my heart race — not in the good way either, but in the panic attack way. Sweat bubbles up on my forehead and the ground tilts so fast I grab the mailbox for support. I hear the counselor's voice in my head telling me panic attacks are common and manageable with the 54321 method and cast my eyes around for five things I can see: the dumb fish mailbox, white paint peeling from the post, a few browning daisies at my feet, clouds scuttling across the sky, a raven flying toward the farm next door.

I count through three deep breaths then focus on four things I can feel: the sun on my face, sweat running down the center of my back, the mail bunched in my fist, my heartbeat slowing down.

I close my eyes and focus on three things I can hear: that same raven calling in the distance, the bus stopping next door at the old Cooper place. I open my eyes and look up the hill in time to see Kate jump down the last step as if she's just escaped from prison. Kate *Cooper*. The old Cooper place! How did I not put two and two together? I watch Kate storm toward her house, and by the time she disappears inside, I realize my panic attack is over.

KATE 1

Mom has her fake happy on when I get home from school. She's smiling out the kitchen window when I get off that big, stupid, yellow tin can of a bus. She isn't brave enough to meet me at the end of the driveway, but in her own way she's waiting for me like she did when I was in kindergarten. I wouldn't let her come into the school even then, but she'd always be right at the front gate, waving as I walked out of school, as if she was afraid I wouldn't recognize her. I was in grade six before she let me walk the three blocks home alone. I don't blame her for hiding inside today. There's nothing she can say or do to ease the misery consuming me.

I drop my backpack in the middle of the hall and kick off my shoes. They don't even get close to the corner where Mom has hers lined up. I can already hear her yell at me when she sees them. It's the same argument we had almost daily before we moved because, as she would say, the entrance in the apartment was too small for one of us to be messy.

"Kate! Your shoes! How many times do I have to ask you not *to leave them in the middle of the entrance where I have to trip over them?"*

"You don't have to trip over them if you don't want to."

Even though I take the time to play this scenario in my head, I still don't bother to bend over and move them. Part of me wants to see how far Mom will let things slide, how far I can push her, and how much she will let me get away with. I still have quite a few pity cards left to play and I'm not above using them.

After a couple of minutes of silence, she peeks around the corner.

"Hi, sweetheart. How was your first day?"

The truth is, the best thing about my day was the fact that I'd negotiated a Friday start with her and have the weekend to recover from the horror of that school. Instead, I say: "Fantastic. I joined the Glee Club."

I don't look at her face. I stomp up the stairs to my room and slam the door as hard as I can. My room! What a joke. It smells like must and old people. The whole house smells like must and old people, with a mix of cat pee. It's disgusting. I fall onto the bed and just about get swallowed by a cloud of dust.

"Katie?" Mom taps at the door. "Can I come in?"

"Whatever. It's your room."

She eases her way inside and I almost feel sorry for her. I know I'm being a nightmare. But what did she expect would happen when she ripped me out of my perfectly dope life and dragged me across the entire country to live in Hicksville?

"I want you to think of it as *your* room now."

She sits down on the edge of the bed and dares to touch my shoulder. It's a tentative touch. I can feel the hesitation in it, like she's afraid I might roll over and chomp her arm clear off her body. I might just, I'm that angry.

"Mom. This is *not* my room. Seriously. In what universe would I hang a poster of David Bowie on my wall?"

She looks at David with nostalgia.

"Maybe this weekend we can redecorate. Would you like that? We can go into town and get some paint. Any color you want. What color would you like?"

I pause for effect. "Black."

Of course, I don't really want to paint my room black. I'm just trying to make a point. To be honest, I'd love to decorate the room and can picture exactly what I want: alternating purple and gold walls, with lots of mismatched cushions and maybe even a red beanbag chair, or hammock. But there's no way I'm going to admit this when I'm in such a foul mood.

Mom looks around her old room and says in a soft voice: "Black might be nice. A bit dark. But if we had the right accents …"

I sit up suddenly and she flinches.

"Mom! I don't want to paint this stupid room. I don't want to live in this stupid house, and I really don't want to go to that stupid school. I hate it here. I hate everything about living here. I just want to go home."

"Katie, sweetheart. It's only been a week. We have to give it a bit more time."

Time? I think to myself. *The first week felt like ten years. How long will another fifty-one weeks feel?* I can feel the anger inside me building, bubbling, boiling. I'm ready to blow.

"I don't understand. I get that you inherited this place from your dead parents. I get that it's worth money. I get that you needed to come back here for some reason I can't grasp. But why can't we just sell it and take the money back home? Why can't we buy a house there?"

"The money from this place wouldn't even buy a one-bedroom condo out west and I'm tired of throwing money away on rent. Besides, we promised to give this move a chance. We promised to give it a year before we make any decisions."

She closes her eyes and pinches the bridge of her nose like she's trying to hold back a flood of tears, or maybe a migraine.

"I didn't promise anything," I mutter.

She doesn't say anything after that. I can see her trying not to get angry and say something she'll regret. The truth is, I want her to get angry. I want a big shouting match. It would feel better if I could scream at her, at the stupid polka-dot bedspread, at the falling down house, and at the hundred acres of isolation stretching out like a wasteland in all directions.

"Tell me about your day. What classes did you get? Did you meet anyone?" Her voice wavers with forced cheerfulness.

I roll my eyes and think about the girls who whispered as I walked down the hall. I think about the boys in my classes who gawked at me for sixty-five minutes of the seventy-minute period. I think about the one boy on my school bus who looked like he wanted to say hi, like he might have introduced himself if I hadn't slouched in my seat and stared at my lap the whole ride home. But I don't think that really counts as meeting someone.

"It was fine. I have English, drama, careers, and math. I met the principal, and later she called me down to the office to find out why I missed math."

"You missed math?"

I don't answer but look out the window. Someone is riding a green lawn tractor up the road, so I concentrate on that while Mom tries to burn holes in my back with her eyes.

"Why did you miss math?"

"I went uptown for lunch and it took an extra seventy minutes before I could muster the courage to go back."

"Kate!"

"What? That school's a joke. Do you know they have a Garden Club?" I snort at the absurdity of a bunch of teenagers getting excited about growing carrots and remind myself to include it in my daily update to Austin.

"Listen. This is an agricultural community. They do things differently here. But it doesn't mean you're better than them."

"Whatever," I mutter and roll my eyes.

"Don't start again, Kate. I'm warning you. If you start skipping classes again ..."

"What? You'll move me to the other side of the country as a punishment?"

Mom ignores this comment and stands up. I hope she'll leave without saying anything more, but she stops at the door and turns around.

"I'm sorry, Kate. I wasn't trying to ruin your life, no matter what you think or how it feels. I love you and it's my job to do what's in your best interest. I couldn't let you keep going on the path you were heading down and this was the only option I had."

I take a deep breath and try to pin a thought into place. Maybe there's still that one thing I haven't said that could change everything. If I could just figure it out. I mean, if we moved back now, I wouldn't even be behind in my classes. And there's a chance I could still fix things. Maybe not with Serena. That friendship is busted like a smashed window. Shattered forever. But I still have Austin.

"Mom! It wasn't my fault. I know you don't believe me. But Serena basically framed me."

Mom holds up her hand and shakes her head. "Let's not do this again. Okay? Let's just give it the year." She pauses, then adds, "Now, what would you like for dinner?"

We've said it all a hundred times, maybe a thousand times. If I had a minute of broadband for every time we had this argument, I'd be able to download the new season of *Shameless*. Twice.

I sigh my defeat. "Did you call about getting the internet hooked up?"

"Yes. They're coming Monday. Be careful with your data until then."

I nod, but I'm not willing to give her too much satisfaction by looking relieved. And there isn't a chance I'm going to say thank you. Part of me feels guilty — I mean, she's actually a pretty good mother and I do love her — but the stakes are too high to give in now. There's still a chance my bad behavior will have us back home by Thanksgiving.

"Mushroom risotto and spinach salad okay with you?"

"Fine. Whatever."

"Come down in a few minutes. It won't take me long."

I listen to her go down the stairs and start cooking. I should follow and offer to help but I don't. Still, my stomach rumbles at the thought of dinner. No matter how much I want to stage a hunger strike and make her as miserable as I feel, there's no way I can miss a meal. My mother's an amazing chef.

I pick up my phone and calculate the time difference in my head. Austin will be heading into third period after lunch, if he didn't skip with the others and hit the food court at the mall. There're no texts but a new photo on Instagram. Austin and Serena are on the benches by the back doors of the high school, the ones by the gym where last year I hung out at lunch with everyone. So they didn't skip. But they're sitting a bit too close together for my liking and Serena is holding a Starbucks cup. Typical. I've been gone a week. If I was a bigger person, I'd hit the heart button and type in a comment like: *Would kill for a Starbucks about now.*

Instead, I turn on the video function and aim my phone at a stain on the ceiling for a few seconds while voicing over a scathing commentary. I wonder if the roof leaked when my mother lived in this room and if she used to stare up at it. I wonder if the roof still leaks. It wouldn't surprise me. The house doesn't look like anyone has fixed anything in about twenty years, or maybe longer. I wonder again about my grandparents, the ones who had lived in this house longer than my mother's been alive, the ones who left their possessions and their smell behind to choke me. I have no memory of either of them, though Mom swears I met them when I was little. If this place is as important to her as she claims, why haven't we visited in, like, forever?

Other than my mother banging around in the kitchen and the faint hum of the radio, the house is quiet. The yard is quiet too, and except for the rumbling tractor driving past, the road is deserted. Actually, the silence of the country creeps me out. I miss the sounds of traffic and sirens, voices, and construction. I sigh. If only I wasn't stuck lying on a squeaky bed, gawking at a brown-stained ceiling.

The sounds of my mother moving about the kitchen stop and my ears perk up. I hear the screech of the screen door and Mom talking to someone on the porch.

I creep over to the window and look out. Beyond the porch roof I can see the back end of the lawn tractor parked in the driveway but I can't see who's driving it.

"Wait 'til I tell Austin people actually drive tractors around here," I mutter under my breath. "This takes Hicksville to a whole new level."

Just then I hear the front door bang closed and Mom climb the first few stairs.

"Kate? Kate, can you come down? Someone's here to see you."

ZACH 2

Dad isn't around when I get home from school, which is pretty typical for him so I don't worry. But I text to see when I should expect him. He texts back saying he won't be home until around 8 p.m. Then, as an afterthought: *Can we eat then?*

Normally I'm starving by dinner, but since I ate the leftover spaghetti when I got home from school, I know I'll be good for a couple of hours. To be honest, I'd mostly texted him because I wanted a distraction from thinking about Kate. But it didn't work. I text back: *Sounds good. CU then.* Then I wonder what to do for the next few hours.

Everyone knows the best way to get a girl's attention is to not try too hard. You've got to act nonchalant, like it's no big deal, right? So, of course, like an idiot, I totally ignore my gut instinct and on impulse ride our oversized John Deere lawn mower over to Kate's house. It isn't until I'm bumping up the driveway that I realize what a seriously bad decision I've made, but what can I do? The tractor is so loud Kate probably heard me coming long before she could see me. Before I can figure a way out of my mess, Kate's mom steps onto the porch and smiles at me. I turn off the tractor and the silence vibrates in my head.

"Hi. Uh. I'm Zach. From next door." I point down the hill toward our place. "My dad said I should come over and cut your, uh, grass." It's a pretty good cover-up. Always blame your parents when you look like a moron.

We both look at the grass. It hasn't been cut for weeks. It's basically hay.

Kate's mom looks uncomfortable and suddenly I feel like a total jerk. What if she likes her grass long? Like, what if she's some sort of environmentalist and is letting it grow for the bees?

I'm about to turn on the tractor again and boot it out of there when she says: "That's very generous of you. And your father."

She pauses again and in that second-long stretch of silence I'm totally at a loss for words. So I just sort of watch the grass grow and wonder if Kate is in the house and what she's doing. I glance at the windows, hoping she might look out. But also hoping she doesn't.

"The lawn's a bit of a mess, huh? This was my parents' place so I'm still figuring some things out. The lawn mower was next on my list."

I brighten. "It won't take long with the John Deere."

It's another lie. They have about five acres of grass. I'm looking at two hours. Minimum.

"Are you sure you don't mind?"

I scratch my ear. What I really want to do is hit myself over the head with a rock for being such an idiot, but I'm stuck. So I smile and say: "It's really not a problem."

"I'm Sally, by the way. Sally Cooper. You might have met my daughter, Kate, on the bus today."

She gives me a kind of all-knowing mom smile, one that says: *I know why you're really here.*

A blush rushes up my face and I try to cover my obvious discomfort with words. "Yeah. We're in the same English class."

"That's nice. It'll be good for her to have a friend nearby. Let me go get her."

My first instinct is to ask the lady what distant planet she lives on, and if she really thinks her daughter was out to make friends on her first day of school. But, of course, I don't say either of those things. Instead, I mumble something about not disturbing her or Kate and getting to the grass, then I start up the John Deere. She waves and yells something at me, but I can't hear over the engine so I just nod back.

I've been cutting grass for about an hour when Kate's mom reappears with a glass of lemonade. We sit together in the shade of the front porch. I take a sip. It tastes gingery and sweet.

"Tough going when the grass is so long," she says.

I nod. "I should have brought the baler."

Kate's mom, Sally, laughs at this. "I have no idea why my father kept so much lawn. Did you know my parents?"

"Not really. We've only been living out here a couple of years."

I keep glancing past her shoulder to the screen door, hoping Kate will make an appearance, that she'll slip out with a shy smile playing at the corner of her lips, her fingers twirling a stray strand of hair like a scene from some old eighties Brat Pack movie that my dad still likes to watch when he's feeling nostalgic.

"Where did you live before?" Sally asks.

"In town. Near the hospital."

"So much has changed since I left. It's bigger."

"They turned the racetrack into big box stores."

"That's right. I remember now. There was one of those towers there. I climbed up once and was too afraid to come down. My boyfriend had to climb up and help me."

We continue to stare down the lawn in front of the house. It's like an eighties haircut — long on one side and short on the other. The silence brings my thoughts back to Kate.

"Are you enjoying being back?"

"Well. It's certainly a big change. I've been away longer than I was here."

"What about your daughter ... Kate?"

Sally laughs. "Not so much. I think if she could hire a hit man to take me out, she would."

She's exaggerating, of course.

"What did you do out west?"

"I owned a restaurant."

"What sort?"

My question seems to surprise her and she fumbles for the words in her head while I sip my lemonade, which is seriously the best I've ever tasted, even better than the stuff they sell fresh squeezed at the fall fair.

"I guess you might call it a bistro. I like to experiment with local ingredients so I changed up the menu a lot."

"Are you going to open a restaurant here?"

"I am. I signed a one-year lease for a space on the main street. It used to be a Greek place."

"Colossus?"

"That's it."

Sally takes my empty glass. "Would you like more?"

"No, thanks. It was really good though," I say and look out at the expanse of green waiting for me.

"Hang on. I called Kate to come down but she hasn't shown her face yet. She's pretending to be on death row, but maybe I can talk her into taking a break."

"Uh, that's okay. She's probably busy," I mutter. "And I should finish the grass."

"Well, I apologize for her, Zach. She's still adjusting to the move. But thanks for coming over and helping out. Tell your parents I owe you dinner when we get settled."

"It's just me and Dad."

"You and your dad then. I look forward to meeting him."

I climb back on the lawn mower knowing I won't catch a glimpse of Kate and realizing that's probably a good thing. I wouldn't want her to associate me with being pissed off, or with a lecture by her mother, or whatever might happen after I leave.

× × ×

When I get home, Dad is on the back deck barbecuing burgers and I try to remember what I did with Mom's postcard. The last time she sent one, I left it on the kitchen counter and he read it. I watched him pick it up and turn it over. His shoulders sort of sagged when he put it down again, and he rubbed the back of his neck the way he does when he's sad. I try to remember if I put the postcard in my backpack or left it on the table then chastise myself. *Maybe try and take better care of your things instead of leaving them all over the house.* It's a mash-up of Dad and Mom both in that thought. I wonder how old I will be when I finally get complete control of my own head.

"Was that you I saw next door cutting the grass?" Dad asks when I open the patio door.

"Trying to be neighborly," I say. "Actually, I said it was your idea."

"What a good idea I had! Why exactly did I have it?"

Because he's a detective, I figure he already knows about our new neighbors, so I tell him about Kate. I mean, I don't tell him everything, just that she's new and living next door and in my English class. He's so involved in what I'm saying, he stops paying attention to the barbecue. I cough on the smoke.

"Uh, Dad? The burgers are on fire."

He grabs his water bottle and douses the flames. We both stare down at the charred meat. "I thought that's the way you like them?"

And he wonders why *I'm* a smart-ass.

"Anyhow, Sally says she's going to invite us for dinner when they get settled. As a thank you for cutting her grass."

"I remember Sally Cooper."

He says her name reverently, like she's some sort of celebrity.

"Seriously? You know her?"

"I met her once or twice, but it's more like I know *of* her."

"Did you go to school together?"

"She might have been in grade nine the year I graduated. She was cute. Even some of the boys in my grade had a crush on her. But she only had eyes for Mitch Goheen."

"Goheen? Like Peter Goheen? The cranky old guy on the second concession?"

Dad nods and flips the burgers, presses on them with the spatula and turns off the gas.

"He has a family?"

Peter Goheen is a bit of a legend in the area, and not in a good way either. Rumor has it he killed his wife and got away with it. Or maybe that's just a story parents tell their kids to keep them from wandering too far from home. Whatever the truth is, everyone's wary of Peter Goheen. He has a reputation for being mean and coldhearted. My friend Josh lives a couple properties away and swears the guy shot his beagle, Daisy, for running across his field. I don't know if I believe the rumor about him killing his wife, or if he really shot Daisy, but Josh was torn up about losing his dog for months. Who wouldn't be? Daisy was the sweetest dog ever. Now he has a different dog, another little hound named Swifer. Holy, that dog can follow a scent.

Dad stacks the burgers on a plate and I follow him inside.

"I'm not sure he sees much of his family but he does have one. A son, at least. Now, tell me about your grass-cutting expedition. Was it successful?"

I dress my burger with ketchup, hot mustard, lettuce, and onions, then take a bite. Other than the burned part it tastes pretty good.

"If you measure success by the amount of grass I cut, then yes, it was successful." I talk and chew at the same time. Mom would scold me for talking with my mouth full but Dad doesn't even notice. He doesn't respond either so I assume he's lost in his own thoughts, perhaps reminiscing about his youth or mulling over something from work. He's a pretty quiet guy for the most part, which means our house is also pretty quiet. It echoes silence, if that's possible.

I think again about the neighbors, about Sally's lemonade, and about Kate tucked away somewhere in the house. *Maybe she was watching TV and didn't know I was there*, I reason with myself. *Maybe she's really shy. Maybe I should give her another chance to come out and say hi.*

"Do you think I could borrow the weed whacker? I was thinking of maybe going back next week and doing around the house and mailbox. I don't think they have much in the way of tools and stuff."

Dad smirks and nods.

"Sure thing, Zach. I bet Sally would appreciate the help."

KATE 2

In the eleven days I've been in Hicksville, I've not looked around the house. I've basically moved between the dusty bedroom, the lavender bathroom, and the ugly green kitchen. The only other place I've been is the barn. I snuck out on our third night to shoot a video and uploaded it to YouTube. Talk about dark. You haven't seen darkness until you've been in the countryside where there're no streetlights or car lights or lights from other buildings. It was pitch black and that part was kind of cool. But my video still got the worst batch of comments ever and only a handful of thumbs-up emojis. One person bet I wouldn't last forty days in the sticks before I'd run back to the city. I wish it was that simple. I'd pay serious stacks of cash for an escape hatch. But what that failed video made me realize is that I have to step up my urbex video game or I'm going to start losing more than just my sanity. I'm going to start losing followers.

Before I leave for school on Monday, I stand at the edge of the living room and glance inside. Maybe I'm looking for inspiration. Or maybe it's desperation. Whatever the reason, the room still makes me gag, and even with Hicksville-level darkness and killer narration, I couldn't turn it into a hit video for my channel.

YouTube videos aside, it wouldn't be as bad if every surface wasn't covered in crocheted doilies and the carpeting wasn't from the eighties, or worse, the seventies. But even the couch and armchairs are older than my mother and everything is covered in dust and cat hair. I mean, seriously, the amount of DNA in the couch cushions alone would be enough to keep a forensic team busy for decades. There are family photos hanging everywhere so I finally take the time to inspect them. I can pick out my grandparents — Gord and Bonnie — and my mother. I even recognize an aunt of my mother's who I think is Aunt Kathy, the person I'm named after. But most of the faces are of complete strangers. I shoot a quick video and think about sending it to Austin, then decide against it. Some things aren't worth sharing.

Mom finds me as I'm leaving the living room and decides it's time to break the silence that has fallen like darkness over the house. I refused to make small talk for most of the weekend and hid out in *her* room trying not to use too much data on my phone. Basically, it was like being in solitary confinement.

"I don't think you were very civil to Zach last week. So I hope you'll make more of an effort today," she says as I walk to the front door and pull on my Vans.

I'd hoped to leave without having to face off with her.

"To who?"

"To Zach. He lives on the next property over? The boy who came and cut the grass on Friday? Hello? The least you could have done is come out and say a few words to him. You can't be rude in a small town or you'll never make any friends."

"I don't want any friends."

She doesn't bite right away, but the set of her shoulders sharpens. I already hate the way her voice will sound when she finally opens her mouth.

"Fine. But you're going to be awfully miserable living out here without any friends for the next eleven months."

"Eleven months, two weeks, and five days." I know I'm pushing a button I shouldn't push, but I can't help myself.

"Speaking of five days, that's how many more days I'm going to put up with this bullshit of yours. Then, *my friend*, it's hardball."

She turns abruptly and stomps up the stairs. When she gets to the top, she slams the bathroom door so hard a framed picture falls off the wall, cartwheels down the stairs, and shatters at my feet. I wait a moment to see what she'll do but she doesn't open the door and apologize. She doesn't run down the stairs to make sure I'm okay. She turns on the shower and, to make it worse, she starts singing.

"*R-E-S-P-E-C-T. Find out what that means to me!*"

I want to be angry but my mom has some pretty serious pipes so all I can really be is impressed.

There are ten minutes before the bus so I grab the broom. I pick the frame carefully from the shards of glass and clean up the mess. There are two pictures pressed together, like someone was too cheap to buy a second frame. I glance quickly at the front picture, which shows a young version of my mother. She's in a graduation robe, holding a diploma. It's one of those studio shots. I'm surprised to see how much of my own face is in hers. Her hair isn't as curly as mine, but there's something about her jawline, about the way her hair sweeps off her forehead, about how her eyes squint into the camera. The alarm on my phone buzzes and words flash across the screen: *Move UR Ass. Bus in 2 Minutes*. I jam the photo, frame and all, into my backpack. Then I run out the front door as the bus pulls up to our driveway.

There are only three other kids on the bus and they are all in the very back, so I have plenty of choices about where to sit. I pick a spot two seats behind the driver without making eye contact with anyone, slouch down, and brace my legs against the seat in front of me.

"Whatcha doing?"

Tractor Boy hangs over the back of my seat, gawking over my shoulder. His hair is long, scraggly, and tucked into a backward baseball cap. He has that casual, but calculated, look I hate in guys. He's too obvious, like he needs constant attention, especially from girls. I glance at him quickly when he looks over his shoulder to the back of the bus. Actually, he looks like the kind of guy a lot of girls would go for, but he's nothing like Austin and definitely not my type.

"Sitting on a bus," I say deadpan. Then I wait, just in case he missed the fact that I have more important things to do than answer his stupid questions.

"Why?"

I don't answer right away because I'm trying to figure out what kind of stupid question "*Why?*" is. I mean, I'm obviously sitting on the bus so I can go to school. I glance over my shoulder and he hasn't moved, is still leaning forward, staring ahead. I second-guess myself, wonder if he's being philosophical, if it's some kind of test. Is he expecting me to say something profound like: *Because I exist?*

"Because I want to," I say finally. But even to my ears, I sound like a bitch. So I clear my throat. "Unless you know a better way to get to school."

He nods knowingly. "I could lend you our riding lawn mower. Gets up to ten miles an hour going downhill."

I can't help myself and laugh, just a little, more like a snort.

"Ah, so you *do* have a sense of humor," he says. Then he sits back with such a self-satisfied look I have to clench my fist to keep from hitting him.

"I probably have a better sense of humor than you. I just don't go around showing it off."

"On the contrary. I'm not showing it off. I'm so funny I just can't contain it sometimes."

"Is there something I can help you with, Zach? If so, just cut to the chase already."

This time it's Zach's turn to pause for effect and he drags it out. I swear to God, he even feigns looking at his fingernails. "And you even know my name?"

"Yeah, so big deal. My mom told me this morning."

"I guess I made a pretty big impact on your mother. She seemed to like me."

"Oh my God! Are you always this annoying?"

"It's part of my charm," Zach says casually.

"Someone told you this was charming?"

Zach ignores the bait and changes the subject. "I was thinking of coming over after school to do the weed whacking. Your mother seems to need the help. Maybe I'll see you then. Or maybe I'll enjoy talking about you with your mother again."

"Wait! You guys were talking about me?" I ask.

I feel my temper spike and I clamp my teeth together to stop myself from saying anything else, from letting him know how bothered I am by his intentionally offhand comment. I can't help but wonder exactly what she said about me. In fact, I want to know more than I want to admit.

But Zach doesn't answer. Instead, he jumps off the bus and slips into the crowd of kids streaming into the school. I stand up and wait. The girl in front of me drops her phone and stops to pick it up while I fume. Zach is easily the most annoying guy I've ever met in my life.

✖ ✖ ✖

The next time Zach shows up at our house he comes by foot, carrying the weed whacker over his shoulder. He walks slowly, with his face down and that terrible hair hanging in front of his eyes. I video him from my bedroom window as he walks up the hill toward our house, then turns into our driveway. That's when I sneak down the stairs and go outside to meet him.

"Hey!" I call out when we're about twenty feet apart.

He squints into the sun and says: "Hey back."

"Where's that sweet ride you had last week? I thought you were going to let me drive it to school?"

He blushes and I feel sort of bad for teasing him. But Zach doesn't miss a beat, which is something I could probably learn to appreciate about him.

"It's at the body shop getting tricked out. I thought flames would be a nice touch. What do you think?"

I can't help but laugh. "That would be totally badass."

I turn and walk with him toward the house. He puts the weed whacker on the ground and looks around.

"You don't really have to do that, you know."

"But I live for weed whacking. It's an honor. In fact, I feel like I owe you for letting me do it."

He kneels down and fiddles with the gas cap in a way that makes me wonder if he actually knows how to use it.

"You're so weird," I say. "But I could actually use your help if you're into chivalry."

He stands up and wipes the hair out of his face, considers the weeds growing tall around the perimeter of the house. The more I look at him, the more he reminds me of someone, but I can't quite figure out who. I scan through my friends from back home but my synapses don't make the connection.

"I'm not going to tell you what your mother said about you so don't even ask."

Now it's my turn to blush and I fumble to speak. "Don't worry. I won't. I forgot all about it actually."

"Likely story. So what do you want me to do? Nothing illegal, I hope."

What I am about to propose is cringeworthy, and if I wasn't desperate, I'd find another way. But I can't take another day of silence in the house, another sullen meal, another rendition of "Respect" by my mother. I mean, I am not over the move, I'll never be over the move, and I haven't given up on *Operation Get the Hell Out of Hicksville*, but I need a couple of days off. It's been a long weekend. And digging in my heels is just making her dig in more.

Zach eyes me suspiciously, then looks down the hill toward his own place, as if I am taking too long and if I don't hurry up and spill it, he's going to walk home.

"It's just … I was hoping … Can you maybe come inside and say hi to my mom? It'll make her happy to see I've made a friend."

Zach turns to face me. He raises his eyebrows in high arcs. "So, I'm a friend now?"

"Sure, I guess. I mean, we just met. But if she sees me making an effort ..."

I don't finish the thought because my brain catches up to my mouth and I hear how *mean girl* I sound. What's worse is I can see how my *mean girl* comment lands. Zach scowls in response, glances down at the weed whacker and over at the house again as if he's decided the weeds look more promising than doing me a favor. I mean, I don't want him to think I'm only using him, because I've been on the wrong end of that equation too many times with Serena before and it doesn't feel good. But I also don't want to commit to anything. After all, I'm pretty sure we have nothing in common and he's the first person I've met. Plus, he seems a little desperate, so who knows, maybe he's the town weirdo and I'm stepping into a trap.

Finally, he says: "What's in it for me?"

It makes me a little bit happy to realize he's not a complete pushover, that he has enough backbone to expect something in return. It's more interesting, you know, when you don't have all the power.

"I'll think of some way to repay the favor," I say. "Just don't answer her questions with too much detail or we'll be there forever."

"Message received."

We step up onto the wooden porch and through the screen door. As soon as it bangs shut, Mom calls out from the kitchen.

"Kate?"

"Yep. Hi. Zach came over for a bit. Hope that's okay."

We walk into the kitchen just as Mom is wiping her hands on a tea towel.

"Zach! Good to see you. I hope you didn't bring the lawn tractor this time!"

Zach blushes for a second time in ten minutes.

"Actually, he brought the weed whacker," I say. "But I suggested he show me around the property instead."

Zach looks surprised but plays along. "That's right. Since we share a property line, I know yours just about as well as mine. I thought I could show Kate the, uh, highlights."

Mom is so happy she practically lights the room up with her smile. It almost makes me feel bad that she's falling so hard for my con. She turns to Zach, who's looking around the kitchen. There's a blender full of raspberries, a colander in the sink draining pasta, canisters of flour and sugar open on the table, jars of spices strewn about. There are three different cutting boards heaped with veggies, measuring cups of freshly chopped herbs, two saucepans and a frying pan on the stove.

"Wait," Zach says. "Is this dinner?" He has a haunted, hungry look about him, like he might drool into one of the mixing bowls.

Mom laughs. "No. No. I'm experimenting with some new recipes. Are you hungry? I made lemon poppy seed cupcakes this afternoon. With cream cheese icing?"

"We're fine," I say as I try to edge us out of the kitchen. Zach resists but eventually follows my lead and scuffles backward.

"Quinoa walnut salad?

"That's okay." I shake my head.

Zach mouths *keen-wa?*

Mom looks disappointed. She loves to feed people and I'm never enough people to keep her satisfied. But she tries again. "Potato pockets with double-smoked bacon and provolone?"

"No thanks." I smile and press Zach to move faster.

"Roast beef sandwiches on rye with horseradish mayo?"

Zach stops moving and looks from Mom to me and back again. "Actually, I wouldn't mind a roast beef sandwich. I mean, I haven't eaten since I got home from school."

I look at the clock on the stove. It's only five, but I don't say anything when I see Mom's expression turn into a smile again, squinty eyes and everything. She gives me that *I told you so* look and rummages through the fridge. Zach shrugs an apology at me and I roll my eyes. Now we're going to have to wait ten minutes for Mom to make him a sandwich. And who knows how many questions she could squeeze into that amount of time.

"Lettuce, Zach?"

"Yes, thanks."

"Pickle?"

"Please!"

"I'll make it to go," Mom says as she cuts it into two pieces with a flourish. She wraps it in parchment paper and hands it to Zach with a can of San Pellegrino.

"Now off you go to do whatever it is you're in such a hurry to do. When you come back you can try one of the cupcakes."

Zach has a dopey smile on his face and I tug the tail of his shirt to get his attention. He thanks Mom about fifteen times and finally follows me outside.

"I'm so jealous right now," he says as he unwraps the sandwich. He takes a bite while we walk toward the barn. "Omigod, this is amazing!"

"Okay, I admit it. She has a way with food."

He takes another bite and moans with delight.

"Get over it. It's just a sandwich," I mutter.

"I'd weigh two hundred pounds if I lived with her."

I look him up and down. With his frame, there's no way he'll ever be two hundred pounds. He'll be lucky to hit one-fifty by his eighteenth birthday.

"What do you want to see first?" he asks through a cheek full of sandwich.

I scowl and shrug. "I don't know. What's there to see?"

"Fields, trees, fences."

"Sounds thrilling," I mutter.

Zach swallows and tilts his head. "What's in the barn?"

I look at the barn mutely. There's no point trying to explain that I was only in the barn for twenty minutes to shoot a video. And there's definitely no point in trying to explain why.

"I dunno. I haven't actually looked around that much. I've mostly been hanging out in my bedroom."

"Part of your protest?"

"Something like that."

We follow an overgrown trail beyond the barn, through the fenced fields and to the top of a hill, which is the highest point for a long way around. The fields are empty. There are no cows or crops, but in the far distance there's a stand of pine trees so perfectly ordered they had to have been planted.

"So this is where my mom grew up. Do you think it's the same as when she lived here?" I ask as I sweep my hand across the view before us.

"Probably more or less. Those trees are probably taller now. And I know your grandfather used to keep cows and grow hay."

Despite the weather forecast, the temperature still hasn't broken so for the eleventh straight day I'm choking on the thick, hot air, so different from the cool breezes we got out west. Zach cracks open his San Pellegrino and offers me the first drink, but I shake my head.

Instead, I pull out my phone and turn in a circle, videoing in all directions. Behind us is our house, the infamous Cooper farm, and to the left, across an expanse of field, is Zach's house and barn. Some parts of the landscape are obscured by trees and other parts by hills. But as I continue turning, I see another farm far in the distance, fronting onto a different road.

"Who lives over there?"

Zach looks uneasy. "Some cranky old guy. A bit of a lunatic. He pretty much keeps to himself. But I think your mom might have known his son. Someone named Goheen?"

My breath catches in my throat and sticks like a ball of dough.

"I think that's my grandfather's place."

Zach looks confused.

"Not Gord Cooper. My *other* grandfather. Mitch Goheen is my father. That must be where his dad lives. I've never actually met him. I mean, I barely see my dad. But I know he used to live near Mom when she was in high school. That's how they met."

Zach glances away and rubs the back of his neck. It's clear there's something he doesn't want to talk about.

"What?"

"It's nothing."

"Just tell me."

"Well, uh, it's just, there're a few unsavory rumors about him. The kind of stories kids tell at sleepovers to scare each other. You know?"

"Actually, I don't know. But I would if you just told me already."

"Okay. But it's probably not true."

"Spill it!" I shout.

"Don't get mad. But, well, I heard he killed someone once." He pauses briefly then rushes through the next sentence. "But like I said, I don't know for sure if it's true."

I turn back to the property in the distance and wonder if the rumor could be true and how I might find out. I wonder if my mother knows the story.

My *other* grandfather's property is tucked back off the road. The Goheen house is a large two-story structure with a curved veranda. There's a long driveway leading up to it, a barn and a couple of smaller buildings further in the distance. From where we stand, it looks like a pretty nice place, or like it might have been. It's hard to connect that place to my father, or what I know about him, which isn't all that much: a few summer holidays and Christmases, birthday cards, texts, the odd telephone conversation.

Zach gazes across the expanse of land at the house for a few minutes. He looks hopeful, nervous, then determined. Finally, he says: "It's probably not true. It sort of sounds made up. You know? Maybe he's just a lonely old man and people started saying shit about him that stuck. Do you wanna maybe ... I mean ... well ... maybe we should go introduce you?"

ZACH 3

As soon as I say the words I'm hit with some pretty serious buyer's remorse. Maybe not buyer's remorse exactly, since I didn't actually buy anything, but that same sinking feeling like when I realize the video game I just dropped two weeks of grass-cutting money on is derivative of versions one through four. I wish I could suck the words back into my mouth, vacuum the idea out of the air and up into my brain. But it's too late.

Kate looks at me with a sideways smirk and says: "I was just about to suggest the same thing."

I pull myself out of the downward spiral of doubt and remind myself this is a good thing. The more time I spend with her, the more time she has to realize I'm a decent guy.

"What?" I ask when her smirk doesn't quit.

"Just surprised. You going all *bad boy* and everything. Wanting to go meet, like, a *murderer.*"

"I didn't say murder. Just that he killed someone. Besides, I thought we already established my badassness with the tricked-out lawn tractor."

"But that was just a joke. This is serious *bad boy* stuff."

I'm not going to lie, hearing her call me a bad boy gives me a bit of a thrill. I know that girls like Kate love a bad boy. But I also know that bad boys don't admit to being one. So instead of attempting to correct her, I just flip the comment off my shoulder, hoping she won't drop the conversation.

But she does. And she switches direction suddenly — in more ways than one. She turns away from me, back toward the Goheen property, and changes topics all at the same time.

"What time do you normally eat dinner?"

"I dunno. Whenever Dad gets home. Like seven most nights. Probably more like eight tonight. Why?"

"You just ate so I know you won't be hungry for at least a couple of hours ..."

I try to interrupt and tell her I'm always hungry but she holds up her hand to silence me.

"... and your dad won't be home for a couple of hours. So, it seems like now might be the perfect time."

She nods toward the property in the distance and I realize she hasn't changed topics after all. Despite my rabbiting heart, I try to act casual while I take long, deep breaths. The last thing I need is to end up zoned out on the ground from a panic attack.

"C'mon," she says and pushes my shoulder playfully. "How dangerous can he be? Like you said, he's probably just a lonely old man. And he's like eighty or something. He probably doesn't even leave his rocking chair."

× × ×

In the end we decide it will be easier to bike over to the Goheen property than to navigate cross-country, so we head over to my place. I lend her my mountain bike, a pretty radical Kona that my mom got me last year for my birthday when she was experiencing fresh spasms of guilt about the whole marriage breakup thing, and I straddle Dad's rickety old Walmart special, which isn't all that bad. Kate examines my Kona and makes some sarcastic comment about riding a lame green tractor when I have a totally sweet bike to ride, and I counter by suggesting she might want to put on some running shoes and jeans before we go biking. But she ignores me and heads down our driveway.

Valley Road is quiet and only a few cars pass, but when we turn north onto the main road, vehicles fly past one after another like a never-ending train. We hug the shoulder and keep our heads down, and I'm grateful it's only a couple of miles until we can turn off at the second concession. We ride to the Goheen mailbox slowly, straining to see up the long, curved driveway, but because of the trees, the house isn't visible from the road.

"Now what?" I ask as we take in the faded *No Trespassing* signs posted every hundred feet along the front of the property. There's a faraway rumble of an engine and the longer we stand, the louder it gets: a car is approaching.

Kate stashes her bike in the grassy ditch and I pause to wonder if that's the best thing to do with a Kona that's worth hundreds of dollars. But I don't have the chance to protest because she grabs my arm and pulls me forward along the gravel driveway. As we round the bend, the house comes into view, redbrick and perched on an incline, which makes it seem taller than it really is. Monolithic. There's a wooden porch that runs across the front of the house and up to a formal entrance that doesn't look used. Instead, we head toward the smaller, covered back porch that's littered with signs of life: muddy boots, a wooden chair, an empty dog dish, a shovel leaning against the wall, a pair of woolen socks stretched out to dry. Kate captures it all on video with her phone. If you ask me, she's a bit obsessed with her phone.

"It's not too late to turn around," I whisper as we step up to the door.

But Kate doesn't respond. Her shoulders are squared with determination and she reaches out to knock before I can stop her. She raps on the wooden door loudly, like a woodpecker that has detected a tasty insect trapped behind the bark of an unsuspecting tree.

We wait for some sign of life from inside but hear nothing. Kate knocks again, louder, longer, more insistent. If Peter Goheen wasn't cranky before, the knocking would be enough to set him off. The noise jangles my nerves and I take a few deep breaths to calm myself, holding for a few seconds at the beginning and end of each.

"Maybe he's not home," I suggest hopefully. "We could come back some other time."

Kate scans the yard and, before she even has a chance to speak, I see the dusty gray pickup truck parked just beyond the house. The rest of the yard is tidy, but not showy. It's utilitarian at best. There are no flower gardens or potted plants, no statues or shrubs, but unlike a lot of farming properties, the place isn't littered with farming implements or broken-down machinery.

Kate steps off the back porch and glances up at the house. She sizes it up in a way that makes me nervous, as if she's considering scaling the wall.

"What if he's inside and fell or something? What if he can't get to the door?"

"Then I think he'd yell for help when he heard the knocking," I suggest.

"What if he hit his head and he's unconscious? What if he had a stroke or something?"

"What if he's gone for a walk? Or is cutting firewood in the back lot?" I counter.

Kate scowls at me and approaches a nearby window. She stretches up on her tiptoes and hangs onto the windowsill.

"Kate, I'm not sure we should be snooping around," I hiss. "Let's come back another time."

But it's like she's gone deaf suddenly. She doesn't respond or even acknowledge I've spoken. Instead, she beckons me to join her at the window.

"Can you give me a boost so I can see better?"

"Kate …"

"Just for a second. What if he's lying on the floor?"

Reluctantly, I join her at the window. I crouch down and interlace my fingers. She places one foot in the cradle of my hands and I lift. She's heavier than I expect and it takes a lot of effort to stand up straight.

"Can you see anything?" I ask, trying not to let my voice sound strained.

"There's no body," she says.

"Can I let you down? Have you seen enough?" I shift my feet and lean my shoulder against the wall for leverage.

"Hold on," she says and captures a quick video.

I wait a few more seconds to be polite, then my arms start to tremble.

"I can't hold you up forever," I groan.

"Hold on."

I'm trying to ignore the pain in my shoulders when I notice a dog barking in the distance. And when I say distance, I don't mean like five farms over. I mean, I hear a dog barking from a few hundred yards away. And the sound is getting closer.

I turn my head in time to see a black lab burst through the trees on the far side of the yard. It runs toward us, and not in a friendly way. Without warning I drop Kate and she lands on her feet beside me, the windowsill even with the top of our heads. The dog, barking and growling, reaches us before we have time to move.

"Hey boy, good boy," I say as I take one small step back.

"What's your name? Hey, buddy?" Kate's talking to the dog like it's a small child, but it keeps barking.

"I thought black labs are supposed to be friendly," I whisper.

I back up until I feel the cool pressure of the bricks against my spine and have nowhere else to go. The dog doesn't stop barking but it doesn't come any closer either. Only when a voice comes from the trees does it turn its head. We follow the dog's gaze to see a man step into view, an old man in camouflage pants and a filthy jacket, carrying a gun and two dead rabbits, which he holds by the ears. His face is covered in gray stubble and tufts of greasy hair stick out from under a faded blue baseball cap.

I swallow hard and Kate sucks in her breath.

"Hunter, get over here!" the man yells.

When the dog returns to the man's side, he orders him to lie down. I'm relieved when the barking stops — but then the man turns his attention to us.

"This is private property. No trespassing. Didn't you see the signs?" His voice is gravelly and he's staring at us with so much contempt my legs feel weak. I open my mouth to speak but there's nothing. He glares at us and I can't take my eyes off the rabbits in his hand. Hunter raises his face and licks a drop of blood from one of the dead rabbits' feet.

"Sorry, sir," Kate says, filling up the awful silence. "We didn't mean to trespass."

"What are you doing here? Snooping around? I've told the police what I know. I've told the reporters what I know," he shouts at us, glowering from under his bushy gray eyebrows.

Neither of us has a chance to speak before he starts shouting again.

"I've told everyone what I know and I'm done telling it. I'm tired of people coming around accusing me of something I didn't do. There's nothing to see. Nothing to find. Now get the hell away from here!"

The man swings the limp rabbits to indicate the direction of the road. Hunter follows the movement of the dead animals with his eyes, sliding his tongue out and over his nose.

When we still don't budge, the man doubles down on his anger.

"Are you deaf? I said you're not welcome on my property. Leave. Now! Get going!" He holds up his gun to make his point.

Kate presses herself tighter against me, but I don't have time to enjoy the moment.

"Mr. Goheen?" I finally manage to squeak.

"What?" he shouts impatiently. It's clear he wants us off his property, like, yesterday.

"This is your granddaughter, Kate Cooper. She wanted to come over and meet you."

The birds stop singing and the air stills; a thin veil of cloud crosses over the sun, lowering the temperature and altering the moment so that it feels like we've stepped into another dimension. When I look closer, I see a defeated old man standing before us, the anger drained out, leaving a hollow shell in its shape.

Maybe I was right and he *is* just a lonely old man — and taken by surprise too. *Maybe we should have called ahead*, I think. I feel Kate react beside me, expand with the anticipation of his softening. She steps forward slightly, only a couple of inches and only with one foot, a toe really, but it's enough to shatter the spell.

KATE 3

The old fart glowers at me, examines me inch by inch, starting from the sandals on my feet all the way up to the hair on my head. At first I think he's going to have a change of heart, maybe offer to sit down and chat. It's not like I expect him to invite us inside for Cokes and cookies, like our across-the-hall neighbor out west did on Sundays. She was old and lonely, and loved to treat me like her granddaughter. But I *am* expecting him to at least show an interest in me, ask me a question about myself, or about my father. But he doesn't. He snarls and stares, and chews on his cheeks like he has a hunk of gristle in his mouth he can't swallow. It gives me the creeps, the way he assesses me, and the longer he takes, the more the goose bumps flash mob my bare arms.

But at least he has stopped yelling.

For about ninety seconds.

"I don't give a *shit* if you're the bloody Queen of *frigging* England. I want you off my property! *Now*."

Apparently, the time it took to size me up helped him redis-cover his fury, and his energy. He waves his arms around; the gun and the rabbits brush wildly past his legs and drops of blood splatter on the ground. The dog starts barking with renewed rage and I don't know whether it's better to run or stay frozen in place. I shrink backward beside Zach, press my hands against the cool bricks at my spine, and take strength from the hard surface.

"If you'd kindly grab hold of your dog," I shout suddenly, with a fury intense enough to match his own, "we'd be more than happy to leave."

Zach tenses beside me but the old guy falters. He probably isn't used to being yelled at, and maybe we share more than a few random genes. I take the opportunity and grab Zach's arm, then drag him down the driveway.

"Let's get outta this hell hole. No wonder my father never comes back," I say, loud enough for the lunatic to hear.

We speed walk away without looking back. Don't get me wrong, I want to look back. I want to look back and see the expression on the guy's face. I want to see a flicker of regret or a wince that might indicate remorse, but I doubt he's capable of either emotion and if he's anything like me, he has a stone-cold expression he can hold for hours.

It isn't until we're back at the road that we dare look over our shoulders. Even then we don't linger. We make sure we're in the clear and grab our bikes from the ditch.

"You're the one who's totally badass," Zach says with undisguised admiration.

"Thanks," I mutter and push my bike down the road.

I don't get on my bike right away but push it parallel to the Goheen property, counting off the *No Trespassing* signs in my head. Zach follows silently at my side and lets me think, which I'm grateful for. What I saw through the window was more than Peter Goheen's living room, it was a glimpse into his life and it puzzled me. As you'd expect, the room was full of outdated furniture — a gold plush couch that was actually cool in a retro sort of way — and oppressive floral wallpaper that was probably fashionable whenever it was hung. But there was also a brand-new flat-screen TV, a glass-topped desk with a high-end laptop, and a bookshelf lined with old-fashioned photo albums, the kind with the plastic sleeves where you'd insert photographs. There was also a series of framed photos above the desk — school photos of my father starting in kindergarten and ending with a graduation photo, presumably from when he finished high school. The photos intrigue me the most. I've not seen many pictures of my father, and especially not when he was a kid. I've seen a couple of photos of when he was an older teenager, ones my mother had in a box in her closet out west. I remember one where he's standing in front of Niagara Falls, and a couple from later, when they got together to have me, back when they were newly optimistic about a future together. But I've never seen a photo of him as a child. I'm glad I shot some video. I want more time to look at those photos, to examine how his face changed over time and see what I can learn about his childhood from those changes. I know I'm not finished with those photos, with that room, with that house, but I tuck the memory into the back of my mind for later.

I stop pushing my bike and turn to Zach. "That was weird, huh?"

"Totally weird. I'm sorry ..." he starts to mutter apologetically, like the whole thing was his fault, some massive error of judgment.

But I don't let him finish. There's nothing I hate more than pity and I can feel it welling up from him, about to spill onto the gravel road.

"What was he saying about the police and reporters? People accusing him of things he didn't do?"

Zach shrugs. "Maybe there was an investigation into his wife's death. Maybe there've been other incidents?"

"But what if people have it wrong? What if he's innocent and people have been harassing him for no reason?"

"I dunno. The way people act when you mention his name, he's bad news. And based on our experience, I don't blame them."

That's when I see a little hound dog running toward us, hugging the side of the road with his nose tight to the ground, veering left and right as it inhales some sort of scent. It looks like a lanky beagle with long ears, but with a smattering of black-and-white spots on its legs. Zach spots the dog at the same time.

"Swifer!" he yells out and drops his bike in the ditch. "Here, Swifer! Here boy."

Zach heads toward the dog, calling back over his shoulder at me.

"That's my friend's dog. He must have gotten loose again. He's a regular Houdini."

Eventually, Swifer notices Zach approaching and veers off the road. He barks, a low mournful howl, and jumps across the grassy ditch. Zach follows and is about to disappear into the forest when I call out: "Wait! What are you doing?"

Zach stops for a moment, but I can hear the dog baying as it moves through the forest, quickly expanding the distance between us and him.

"I have to grab Swifer and get him home."

I point at the *No Trespassing* sign beside him. "It's still *his* property. I don't think that's a good idea."

Zach looks at the forest, then back at me. He shakes his head sadly. "I can't leave Swifer alone in there. Josh already lost one dog. C'mon."

Zach disappears into the dark, damp, tightly packed thicket of cedar trees and I drop my bike in the ditch to follow.

The Goheen property flanks Haffy Creek to the east, which means much of the land is low-lying and swampy. From there it rises toward the house, barn, and other outbuildings. But because of the dense cedar forest, it's next to impossible to walk in a straight line.

"What do you mean he lost one dog?" I ask as I catch up and fall in behind Zach.

"Josh thinks Peter Goheen shot his dog, Daisy, last winter. A cute little beagle. If we leave Swifer in here alone, who knows what will happen. I don't think Josh can handle another loss right now."

Zach stops and we listen. The baying stops for a moment, then starts up again and we follow the sound. As much as I wish I was anywhere but in the middle of the forest on my grandfather's property, I tell myself, in Dory's voice: *Just keep walking. Just keep walking.*

"Do you even know where you're going?" I ask as we crawl through a tangle of trees, swipe branches out of our faces, and clamber around stumps and hunks of limestone rock.

"Shhhhh," he says without slowing. "He's probably chasing some animal."

"Should we call for him?"

"No way. If your … uh … grandfather finds us out here, he's going to be beyond mad."

"Hopefully he's inside by now, cooking those rabbits."

We haven't gone far before I notice multiple red welts across my thighs and a trickle of blood running down my shin. Zach is wearing running shoes and jeans but I'm in mall-shopping shorts and leather sandals. I'm not exactly dressed for crashing my way through a forest.

I stop and rub away a line of blood that's tracking toward my ankle.

"Are you okay?" he asks, glancing down at my legs.

"I don't think I'll bleed out or anything, but it doesn't look so great."

"Looks okay to me," he says and his cheeks flush.

I don't comment but go back to scrabbling through the forest. Swifer barks every now and then, just enough to keep us going in the right direction.

The further away from the road we get, the higher we climb and the more the forest changes. The thick, fragrant cedars give way to taller, lighter maples and beech trees, which makes walking easier. Suddenly the land rises sharply and I head for the high point, weaving my way through boulders and branches. When I come to a limestone ledge, I hoist myself up.

When Zach climbs up beside me, he turns and scans the forest and we both listen. But the forest is still, except for the scurrying of a squirrel as it runs up a nearby tree then scolds us for getting too close. It seems my grandfather's not the only one who's territorial. That's when I notice a crack in the limestone, a narrow opening. I step close and lean down to peer inside. A puff of cool air meets my face.

"Look! Zach! It's a cave."

Zach crouches beside me and we peer through the narrow opening together.

"Actually, it's called a crevasse. They're everywhere around here."

The crevasse is dark inside and we can't see further than a few inches. I follow the fissure in the rock until it takes me down the far side of the ledge.

"Zach! Check this out!" The excitement makes my heart thump and Zach leaps down beside me with a thud.

I scowl and motion for him to keep quiet. Then I point at another opening, this one at the base of the rock and large enough to squeeze through. I swipe the flashlight function on my phone and peer into the opening, but still, I can't tell how large the space is or how far down it goes. I pick up a stick and toss it in. A few seconds later I hear it land.

"That's a big cave," I say. "We should check it out!"

Zach listens for Swifer but, hearing nothing, lies down next to the opening and flashes his own phone around the space.

"What can you see?"

"There's a big drop, then a ledge. But I don't think we can reach it without a rope."

I lie down next to Zach until my head is hanging over the opening. He's right. There's no way we can lower ourselves without falling, unless we had a rope to rappel ourselves over the lip of the opening. I sit up when I hear a rustling sound nearby. Zach hears it at the same time and we both look over in time to see Swifer nosing his way through last year's dead leaves.

"Swifer!" Zach calls gently and crouches down with his hand out. "C'mere boy. You want a treat?"

When Swifer notices Zach, he rushes forward, all floppy ears and wagging tail. He almost knocks Zach over with his enthusiasm. It's actually pretty adorable.

"Do you have hold of him?" I ask and approach quietly.

Zach takes off his belt and loops it through Swifer's collar. When I lean down to say hi, Swifer licks my face until I giggle. I'm glad we didn't let him run away. We probably saved the little guy's life.

"C'mon. Let's get out of here," Zach says when I stand up and wipe the dog slobber from my face. He looks in the direction of my grandfather's house. "We really don't need to see that guy twice in one day."

"Or twice in one life," I suggest and follow Zach back through the forest, with Swifer leading us enthusiastically toward the road.

"We can drop Swifer off at Josh's then ride home. It won't take long."

✕ ✕ ✕

When we get back to Zach's we put the bikes in the garage. He stares at the bright red scratches on my legs so I look down too. It looks like someone got out of control with hashtags and used my body to post messages on some social media app. Or more accurately, it looks like I was in a fight with a thorn bush and came in second. There's a long smear of blood down my right shin that I try again to wipe away.

"You look pretty messed up."

I nod and wipe the hair from my sweaty forehead. I need to clear my mind and come up with a good explanation for what we've been doing before I go home to the Queen of Twenty Questions.

"You want to come in and get cleaned up? Maybe have a drink?"

The inside of Zach's place is like a frat house, the way they depict them in movies at least. It's a shamble of magazines and dirty dishes, unopened mail and crushed soft drink cans. But it's also suffering a crisis in terms of style. There're modern plastic bar stools at one end of the kitchen, and at the other there's a cast-iron stove that looks like it was left over from the pioneer days. He must notice me sizing things up because he says: "My parents are complete opposites."

"Your mom's a traditionalist?" I ask as I eye a dusty wooden bowl at the center of the debris-strewn table.

He shakes his head. "Dad."

Zach rummages around the fridge then brings me ginger ale in a mason jar. Bubbles spiral up through the golden liquid and ice cubes clank against the glass.

"Cheers," I say and raise it in the air.

"Sorry you lost the lottery when it comes to grandfathers."

"Not your fault. But it does help explain why my life is so dysfunctional."

I sip the ginger ale and replay the events in my head. Zach sits down on one of the plastic stools beside me and downs half his ginger ale in one gulp. Then he gets up and grabs a box of Ritz crackers, which he eats three at a time. He offers me the box and I take one to be polite, though to be honest, I'm a bit of a home-baking snob.

The room falls into one of those awkward silences that rises up when nobody knows what to say next.

"Where's the washroom?" I ask finally.

He points toward the far end of the kitchen. "Past the coat cupboard."

The washroom is small, just a toilet, a sink, and a window

overlooking the backyard. I wash my face and study it, wet, in the mirror. A drop of water runs down my nose and an image of my grandfather rises up in my mind. I shudder. Do I have his eyes? His forehead? Am I doomed to live out old age with a rabid-mad dog after driving away my entire family with my violent temper? What really happened to my grandmother? I'll have to remember to ask my father next time I talk to him, whenever that might be. I wipe my face with a hand towel. It looks clean and smells of laundry soap and this surprises me. I didn't expect a couple of dudes to be keeping fresh hand towels in the powder room when they clearly aren't so keen on good housekeeping. There's a quiet knock on the door.

"Kate? Your legs are pretty messed up. You wanna borrow something to cover them?"

I open the door. Zach has a pair of folded gray track pants. He hands them to me like a peace offering.

"They'll probably fit okay. And they're clean."

I look at Zach's lanky frame and narrow hips, then down at my legs. He's right, I need to keep them covered for a few days until the welts heal. I take the track pants and smile. It's a sweet gesture.

I haven't said anything to Zach, but I already know I *have* to go back to that cave somehow. I have to go down into that crevasse and make the most badass video ever. I've never been in a cave and have no idea what's in there or what we might find. But I do know this is the only chance I have to win back my fan base on YouTube.

When I return to the kitchen, Zach has an unsettled look on his face, like he's not sure what I'm going to do next and he's not sure he wants to find out. I tuck a strand of hair behind my ear and smile to lighten the mood.

"How do you feel about going back to that cave sometime?"

"Crevasse," Zach corrects me, pauses, then says, "Why?"

"I promise to tell you. Soon. But right now I need to get home. Just remind me to wear some heavy-duty combat gear next time."

✗ ✗ ✗

Mom's in the kitchen searing beef medallions when I get home. There're two plates on the table, already covered with mixed greens, baby shallots, and paper-thin slices of beet. Her forehead is wrinkled with concentration, but she turns when she hears me come through the front door.

"Ahhh, you're back. Is Zach with you?"

"Nope. He went home."

"Dinner's like two minutes away so grab the milk and sit down."

She turns with the frying pan and slides the medallions onto the bed of greens. My stomach growls in response. It's almost eight and all I've had since lunch is a cracker and a ginger ale. I sit at the table.

"Zach seems like a nice guy. Those his track pants?" She places a plate in front of me.

Leave it to my mother to never miss a beat and never beat around the bush.

"Oh, yeah. We went over to his place and got messing around with the hose. My shorts got wet."

"Nice of him to lend you something."

Mom slices a bite of beef, puts it in her mouth. She chews slowly.

"Needs more garlic. What do you think?"

I take a bite, chew quickly, and swallow. "It's good. Is it for the menu?"

"Maybe," Mom says, then gets lost in her thoughts again.

"So, I was curious," I say as I tuck a bite of beet into my cheek and keep my face turned down. "Did you ever meet Dad's dad?"

Mom looks up sharply and her eyes narrow.

"Of course. I thought my dad was bad news, but Peter Goheen is a psychopath. And I'm not just saying that in a conversational way. I know you probably think it'd be nice to meet him or something but promise me you'll stay clear of him."

I chew and swallow, then fill my mouth with a slice of beef medallion.

"I'm serious, Kate. I hate that man. There's a reason your father never visits."

"I won't go near him. I promise."

Mom slices a little harder and stabs at her greens. I've apparently hit an exposed nerve.

"What about Dad's mom? What happened to her?"

"She died when he was little, before they moved here. Some sort of hunting accident. Allegedly."

"Allegedly?"

"I wouldn't put anything past that man. Pure evil."

"But Dad turned out okay."

"Did he? A grown man who can't stay in one place for more than a few months? Can't hold down a job? Incapable of forming meaningful relationships? Incapable of maintaining a relationship with his own daughter?"

"To be fair, we don't live on the same continent," I say quietly through a mouthful of beef. "I mean, maybe if he lived nearby we'd see each other more."

"Don't count on it. Listen. I don't want to come between you and your dad. I want you to have a reliable connection with him. But I don't want you to get hurt either. I don't want you to set your expectations too high."

"Don't worry. You've made sure I don't have a single strand of expectation when it comes to him."

"That's not fair ..." she starts to say.

But I put down my fork and pull out my phone. I'm being intentionally dismissive as I scroll through my contacts until I find his number. I can see we haven't spoken in two months. I push back my chair and stand up.

"What're you doing?" Mom asks.

"I'm going to call him and tell him we moved. He probably thinks we're still out west."

"Kate!" Mom calls out before I disappear through the kitchen door.

× × ×

I pace the freshly mowed grass between the house and the barn while I listen to the phone ringing and my heart pounding. Finally, the ringing stops, replaced by dead air, then a crash and a profanity.

"Shit. Hello? Kate?"

It's obvious I've woken him up, wherever he is. I'm not very good with time zones at the best of times, and besides, I never know where he's going to be when I do call: India, Thailand, New Zealand. Those have been his most recent locations.

"Is everything okay?" he asks, his voice clearing as his mind is pulled into the moment.

"Yeah. I'm fine. Where are you?"

"Australia. Gold Coast."

"Cool. How is it?"

"Gorgeous. I'm renting a little flat near the beach."

"Surfing?"

"You bet. So what's up?"

"I wanted to let you know we moved."

"You moved? When?"

"Eleven days ago. You'll never believe it, but Mom dragged us back to Hicksville." I use the pet name he uses for Mom's hometown.

"You're kidding?"

"I wouldn't joke about something as tragic as this."

"How is it?"

"Small and creepy. We're living in her parents' house. Grandpa finally kicked the bucket, by the way."

"I heard …" His voice drifts off and in the background there's a dog barking. "Are you staying there? Like, for a while?"

"Mom says we'll give it a year and decide from there. Only like fifty more weeks to go."

"I'm sorry, Kate."

"Yeah, well, it's okay, I guess. Anyhow, listen, what I really called to say is that I met your father."

The phone goes silent and in the empty space all I can hear is my own breathing and a plane droning in the distance beyond Zach's house.

"You what?" The alarm in his voice is palpable.

I turn away from the house, in case Mom is listening and by some miracle can hear my conversation.

"Yeah, not really Grandfather of the Year material, huh?"

"Kate. Please stay away from him. I know I have no right to ask anything of you. But … please. There's stuff you don't know … about him."

I snort. "There's everything I don't know about him. Or your mother. Did she die in a hunting accident for real? That's what Mom says."

"Something like that, apparently. I don't really remember. I was only like twelve."

"Twelve? That's only three years younger than me. And you don't remember?"

"I don't know. Maybe I was ten. It doesn't really matter. Just promise you'll stay away from him. Your mother should never have moved you back there. Not while he's still alive. But she did. So you have to promise me you won't go anywhere near him. Okay? Please? Promise?"

The pleading in his tone is so raw it sends a shiver up my back and I tremble in the warm fall air. I grip the phone, stare at the barn, and wonder what to say next.

ZACH 4

The best thing about our high school is the cafeteria. It has an outdoor courtyard off one side that's full of picnic tables. There's even a tree decorated with LED lights. When the weather's nice, I like to eat out there, and when the weather bites, at least I get to look out at it. Josh and I usually eat there because it's not crowded like the caf and it's not stuffy like the hallways. I'm sitting with Josh when Kate appears on the other side of the courtyard. She glances around, steels her shoulders, lifts her chin, and sits down by herself. Then she pulls out her phone and videos a quick 360-degree shot.

"Kate!" I call out before she has a chance to unpack her lunch. I wave my hand in the air, just high enough for her to see me. She turns toward me and scowls, and for a moment I have a sick feeling in my stomach. *What if she pretends she doesn't see me? What if yesterday's adventure doesn't translate into being friends at school? What if I was supposed to know I'm good enough to hang around with in a forest, but never in public?*

But my moment of self-doubt is wasted because when she sees me, she picks up her things and comes to our table.

"Hey," she says when she sits down.

"Hey," I say. "You weren't on the bus this morning?"

"Mom dropped me off. She wanted to talk to the principal about me missing math on Friday."

Josh shifts in his seat to remind me he's expecting an introduction, even though Mrs. P technically introduced Kate last Friday. I clear my throat and muster as much self-assurance as I can.

"Kate, this is Josh. He's in our English class. Also, Kate was with me when we found Swifer and brought him home."

Josh looks at Kate and smiles. "Thanks for that. He got out of his run. If you guys didn't bring him home, I don't know if he'd have ever found his way back."

Kate smiles and my normally chatty friend turns into a statue.

"Kate moved into the house next door to us. The *Cooper* farm," I stress, in case Josh is as thick as me and hasn't put the facts together.

Kate nods and Josh does the same before looking down at his plate and becoming hyper-focused on his French fries. I get what's going on. Kate can be a little bit intimidating up close.

Kate chews on her lip and gazes past me. The sun is shining through her hair, lighting up strands of gold, and leaving her face in a slight shadow. I try not to be a total creep and stare, but it's hard to look away.

Finally, Josh musters some courage, or something, because he swallows a mouthful of fried potato and ketchup and says: "So how do you like our ... uh ... school?"

I cringe and glance sideways to monitor Kate's expression, afraid her contempt for Clarendon will be obvious. But Kate has an excellent poker face.

"It's a bit different than what I'm used to. And I'm sure it's going to take me some time to adjust, but so far so good," she says and smiles politely.

Josh nods and mumbles something about moving from downtown Toronto and how hard it was for him to adjust, but now he can't imagine living in the city. Then he shoves four fries in his mouth and makes an effort to chew them thoroughly before swallowing. Kate looks unconvinced.

She turns back to me. "Have you always lived around Clarendon?"

I nod. "Yep. My dad grew up here. Mom moved here after they married. But she's only from a couple of towns over so it's basically like I've been from here since before I was born."

I can feel other kids staring in our direction, wondering why Kate's sitting at a corner table with a couple of dudes like us. She's clearly someone who could be sitting at the center of the action, at the cool kids' table, on a throne, adored by the masses. I'm self-aware enough to realize this type of thinking is doing nothing to boost my confidence so I'm desperate to change the tone of our conversation. I mean, the universe works on the law of attraction, right? Thoughts create reality and all that?

While I'm busy analyzing the nuances of our tanking conversation, Kate saves the day. "Sorry about your dog?"

Josh looks confused and I realize this is the only thing Kate knows about him, that she's trying her best to have a normal interaction. If I thought she was the coolest girl before, now I'm doubly convinced.

She clarifies. "Zach said she went missing or something? Daisy?"

Josh's expression relaxes and his shoulders drop away from his ears. He sits up a little straighter and shifts to face Kate.

"Thanks. She was a great little dog. Our creepoid neighbor shot her."

I wince inwardly. Everyone knows it's one thing to criticize your own family but not okay for someone else, someone you've just met, to do it. But if Kate is offended, she doesn't let on, and Josh continues, as he tends to do when he gets on a rant.

"He's such an asshole. You'll know him by his dusty old pickup truck. You see that truck and look out! One time he came to our house and complained that my snowmobile was too noisy, from like a mile away. He and my dad ended up in a screaming match in the front yard."

When Josh finally stops for a breath, Kate says: "Thanks for the warning."

"Kate's mom is opening a restaurant in town," I interject, to give them a more neutral topic.

"Oh yeah?" Josh says.

They talk a little about the restaurant and about Kate's old school. They seem to be in a safe groove so I chew my sandwich and let the moment unfold. I'm only half listening to their conversation and trying to think about how to keep Kate at our table for as long as possible when the worst possible thing ever happens: Andrew Morton saunters into the courtyard and heads for our table. There's no mistaking his intent and I'm not exaggerating when I say *saunter*. Andrew Morton does not just walk like everyone else. He has swagger without even trying. His self-confidence turns heads and the courtyard goes silent while everyone watches to see what will happen next. I'm no psychic, but I already know what's coming.

"Kate!" he calls out from a few feet away.

She looks up and smiles, then stands and picks up her books and lunch bag.

"Sorry guys. I'll see you later, okay?"

Then she and Andrew walk away together. Everyone resumes eating and talking, and the balance of the universe is restored. I don't want to watch them walk away, but I can't help myself. It's like when people can't help turning their heads when they drive by a car accident, even though they might see something they'll later wish they hadn't.

Before they leave the courtyard, Andrew must say something funny because Kate laughs. She doesn't just smile. She throws back her head and laughs. It just about shatters my heart.

Josh is concerned when he sees my expression change from annoyance to crushing disappointment and vengeance, all mixed together.

"What? What?" He turns to look at what's captured my attention. Then he shakes his head. "Get over it, dude. You never had a chance. She's way too cool for us."

I chew the last half of my sandwich and feel defeat replace the blood in my veins while I listen to Josh go on about some retro video game console he saw on a Facebook Buy and Sell page that comes with a box of games — all in mint condition.

"It's at some guy's house across town in the Escarpment Estates but ..." he says.

"So why don't you buy it? We could walk there and back in forty minutes."

"It's a hundred dollars."

Josh is a great guy but he's so predictable. He talks forever about wanting something, and then when it's within his grasp, he wants something else. I'm beginning to think it's the dream that's important to Josh. But after seeing Andrew flirt with Kate, I feel reckless.

"Let's go check it out. It sounds like a lot of cash, but if you saved your lunch money for like a couple of weeks, you'd have it paid off."

"What am I supposed to do for lunch?"

I take my empty lunch bag from where it's sitting beside me on the bench and drop it on the table. Josh looks at me, his expression blank — on purpose.

"Let's go get the stupid thing so you can stop talking about it," I say.

That's all it takes, a bit of edge and Josh is stuffing the last of the ketchupy fries in his mouth. In two minutes, we're dumping our garbage in the trash bin and heading out the back door. If we hurry, we'll only miss part of third period, which is so much easier to explain to the office than missing a whole period. We can worry about the consequences later.

When Josh and I get back to school forty minutes later with the 1982 Atari 5200 SuperSystem, complete with two 360-degree joystick controllers and twenty fully functional, mint condition games, the big news is that Andrew Morton dumped his girl-friend, Sadie, and she's in the girls' change room crying. The school is literally vibrating with the news.

× × ×

When I get on the bus at the end of the day, Kate smiles at me.

"You want to sit here?" she asks and slides across the vinyl seat until she's pressed up against the window.

I glance toward the back of the bus where Josh is throwing me a look begging caution, but I don't hesitate. How can I be cautious when my heart keeps pumping out hope? I slide in beside her. As usual, she has her backpack on her lap like a shield.

"Where'd you guys go this afternoon?" she asks. "When Mrs. Purvis asked about you, Sydney said she'd seen you at lunch so of course Mrs. Purvis called the office and there was a whole thing."

"Josh wanted to go look at a video game console so I went with him."

Kate laughs a little. "You ditched school for a video game?"

"Not just *any* video game," I clarify. "A retro video game console, joysticks, and *twenty* mint condition games. Just don't tell my dad. You know, him being a cop and all."

She giggles, which makes my heart pump an extra pint of blood in one squeeze. I suddenly feel more relaxed, like maybe it's not a lost cause.

"I promise I won't tell your dad. But I figure he already knows."

"So what did Andrew Morton want? To show you his athletic trophies?" I ask with maximum sarcasm.

Kate laughs out loud and says, "Something like that." Then she pauses and scowls. "You're not a fan, huh?"

I smile grimly. It's the moment to choose the high road or the low road. I decide on the cow path. "Maybe more of a fan than Sadie Albright is."

The scowl returns to Kate's face. "I can tell you one thing for sure. Sadie's better off without him."

"He's not good company?" I ask with mock surprise.

"It's exhausting having to prop up an ego that size," she says, then reaches over suddenly and grabs my phone. Despite me protesting, she flicks through it.

"You really should have a password. What if your dad started snooping?"

"He doesn't know how to use it. Besides, it's always with me."

I lean over and see she's checking out my games.

"This one's my fave," she says. "There's supposed to be an upgrade in October."

She fiddles some more and I resist the urge to grab it out of her hand. To tell the truth, I'm feeling a little violated.

"You've got some cool tunes," she says before handing it back.

"So I pass your inspection?"

"Yep. You'll do," she says and smiles. Her teeth are so cute I feel weak with emotion.

There's another gap in our conversation while I search my vacuous brain for something clever to say in return, but all I can come up with is her lawn.

"I left the weed whacker at your place yesterday."

"Yeah. I noticed when I tripped over it this morning. Mom put it on the porch. She said she's going to bring it down to your place and say hi to your dad and stuff. You know, be a good neighbor and all that."

I stare past Kate, out the bus window where farms appear and disappear from behind stands of trees, around bends in the road, beyond hills.

"It's okay," I say. "I can come up and get it tonight. Maybe finish what I started for a change." Another echo from my past, the kind of comment my mother directed at my father.

"You don't have to do that. Really. You should save your energy."

"Save my energy?" I ask.

"Yeah. For the bike ride back to check out the cave." She pauses. "Or *crevasse*. Whatever."

I'd half hoped she'd forgotten about that but of course she didn't and now I feel a surge of curiosity.

"You're going to explain your interest in caves at night?" I remind her.

Kate stands up and I'm about to ask her where she's going when I realize the bus driver has taken the reverse route today and we're stopped at her house.

"Text me a time to meet and I promise to reveal all." She laughs, then disappears down the steps of the bus.

I'm feeling so satisfied that she said to text her — and that at least four other people might have overheard — that I forget to panic until the bus starts to pull away. I stand up and fiddle with the latches on the window, swear under my breath, and finally slide it open.

"I don't know your number," I call out.

She points at her phone then turns and continues down the driveway. That's when I look at my phone to see she's programmed her number under *The Girl Next Door*. My heart beats like a bass drum, so loud and steady I'm sure the bus driver can feel the vibration from the front seat.

While I am marveling at Kate's smooth moves, a text flashes across my screen. It's from Josh.

If UR gonna ditch me for a girl I guess I could live with it being that one.

Then a second text arrives with a URL that links to a YouTube channel called *When You Dare to Date Kate*.

KATE 4

It's well past midnight when my phone buzzes. I check to see if it's Austin or one of my other friends from home, who always seem to forget I'm in a different time zone. But it's not and my heart sinks a little when I see it's just Zach. I mean, I'm expecting his text, but I haven't heard from Austin in too many days to not be concerned about the status of our relationship. I push thoughts of Austin from my mind and text Zach to say I'm on my way down.

I pull on a pair of jeans and a black hoodie then tiptoe down the stairs. As quiet as I try to be, they groan like my dead grandparents rolling over in their graves and I'm sure Mom's going to call out. But she doesn't, and I know I'm in the clear when I hear her snoring lightly from her bedroom.

The front door squeaks as I slip outside into the darkness. That's when I freeze. Despite making a series of urbex videos at night, I'm still not a big fan of the darkness at the best of times, which is when there're streetlights throwing down cones of light all around me. But out in the wilds of Hicksville, it's seriously black, punctuated only by the prying eyes of a million stars overhead.

I creep around the house to where Zach and I agreed to meet

and scan the blackness for his shape. But it's impossible to see anything other than the faint, hulking outline of the barn. I stop for a moment and look into the distance. I can see the porch light on Zach's house twinkling across the field and the sweep of car headlights on the next concession, but nothing more.

"Zach?" I whisper. Then a little louder: "Zach?"

"Right here," he hisses back.

I almost jump out of my skin when I realize how close he is.

"What the hell? Don't sneak up on me like that," I scold.

"On the contrary," he says. "I've been sitting in the same place for ten minutes. You're the one doing the sneaking."

I reach out and feel his hand reaching for me. Our fingers meet and a shot of electricity runs up my arm. I pull it back to my side and order my heart to chill out.

"You might have warned me you were sitting there," I complain. My neck is flushed hot with embarrassment and suddenly I'm thankful for the darkness.

Zach clears his throat before speaking. "I didn't know you were close until I heard your voice."

"You didn't hear my footsteps?"

"All I can hear is my brain telling me I should be in bed."

"Whatever," I hiss. "Let's get going."

"Wait." Zach puts his hand on my arm and another zap of electricity surges up into my shoulder. "When were you going to tell me you're a YouTube celebrity?"

"I wouldn't say *celebrity*," I say, secretly pleased with his choice of words.

"What would you call twenty thousand followers and sponsored ads?"

"Luck?"

"Yeah, right," he says, then adds, "I love the one in the old high school lab. The jars of pig fetuses were super creepy. Especially at night, lit up by flashlights."

"That was my breakout video. The first time I cracked ten thousand followers."

"So do you have a script or something? Like for tonight?"

"I'll explain when we get there. You just have to follow my lead. But we really need to get moving."

Zach stashed the bikes midway between our houses, so we climb on those and retrace our previous journey. It's disorienting riding in the dark to start, but eventually I find my balance. I concentrate on the sound of our tires crunching gravel and squint ahead, trying to focus on the lighter shade of gray that defines the shoulder of the road. Zach calls back to me every few minutes. Things like *you okay?* and *still with me?*

"I'm fine," I reply with a slight tone of contempt, although secretly I'm glad he's keeping track of me. I know for sure none of my friends at home — especially not Austin — would have agreed to sneak out in the middle of the night to ride bikes three miles down a country road. They were all up for breaking into abandoned buildings, but not if it meant making too much effort to get there. I'm not sure Austin would even understand why I want to go down into that cave.

Zach stops pedaling and climbs off his bike. I ram into the back of him by accident and he turns to shush me.

"I think there's a car coming," he says, then drops himself and his bike into the ditch.

I quickly follow his lead and flatten myself into the overgrown gully before the car crests a rise in the road. Its headlights brush the handlebars of my bike and I gasp, but I don't dare move or breathe until it passes without slowing. There's no way a couple of kids hiding in the ditch in the middle of the night won't result in a call to the police.

When we climb out of the ditch, my left side is wet and so is Zach's, but we don't stop to complain. We jump on the bikes and pedal twice as hard to make up for lost time.

"Let's take the other way when we go home," Zach calls back to me. "I don't want to do *that* again."

We're standing on the side of the road a few hundred yards from my grandfather's mailbox, contemplating the dense forest that one night ago hadn't seemed as sinister, when Zach rummages in his backpack and hands me a headlamp. I cinch it tight around my forehead, flick it on, and shine the beam of light at the wall of trees. Instead of lighting a path, it only illuminates the first few trees and makes the night feel even deeper and darker.

Zach jumps across the ditch, then shines his light back in my face.

"You coming?"

"Eyes!" I say, shielding my face with my outstretched hand. "*Eyes!*"

He tilts his head and aims his light at my feet instead.

With one quick leap, I join him on the far side of the ditch, then move close to him. I think for sure he's going to tease me for being such a wimp, but instead he reaches back and takes my hand. We squeeze in unison, then set off. Eventually I turn off my headlamp and follow Zach's lead. We weave through the trees as silently as cats. Or at least that's what I imagine. It's more likely that we sound like a couple of drunk buffalo. The darkness swallows our single beam of light and I glance over my shoulder every few steps with a spine-length shiver. For some reason, the forest is ten times creepier than a city at night. And for all of its darkness, the forest is not quiet. The night is thick with the rhythmic sound of croaking frogs and the thrum of crickets, a steady traffic-like sound that fills my head and calms my nerves, until one of us steps on a branch and sets my heart racing.

"You sure you want to keep going?" Zach asks more than once when we stop to track our progress on his phone.

"I'm sure," I say, even though I'm also kind of wishing I was back in bed with Mom's David Bowie poster watching over me.

Twice, I stop and video our progress through the dense forest, commenting on our mission and the feel of the forest at night.

"I know this is a bit different than my usual adventures," I say into the camera, my eyes glowing green, "but stick with me. Maybe it's the start of a whole new genre of nighttime exploration."

I stop walking while the recording continues. "Did you hear that?" I whisper at my phone. "I swear I just heard something. Zach!" I call out in a strained whisper. "Did you hear something?"

Zach stops and turns, his beam of light washing over me and illuminating my face. I try my best to look terrified and whisper as if my phone is my best friend. "My heart is totally pounding right now. I'm so freaked out."

Zach plays along and flashes his headlamp around the forest while we creep further through the trees. I imagine Austin watching my video in a few days and part of me hopes he feels the way I do when I see pictures of him cozied up to Serena on his Instagram page. A bit of jealousy might not be a bad thing. Eventually, I press pause and we continue on for real.

It feels like we've walked for hours before we find the rock outcrop and climb around to the far side. When I check my phone, though, it's only been forty minutes since we left my house. Time has a way of distorting when you're sneaking through the pitch black onto the private property of your psycho, and possibly murderous, grandfather.

"This is it," Zach says as he flashes a beam of light down into the crevasse. "You're sure about this?"

"Stop asking if I'm sure," I snap. Then more softly: "Did you bring the rope?"

Zach drops his backpack and pulls out a length of purple-and-blue-flecked rope. He unwinds it and ties one end around the trunk of a tree. The other end he drops down into the black hole and it falls with a wave and a flick, like a long, angry snake.

"Ladies first?" he asks.

"Screw chivalry. I'll take up the rear."

I video Zach as he lowers himself feet-first through the opening and the limestone swallows him up until only his neck and head are visible.

"There's a ledge about five feet down, on the left. You should be able to reach it," he says, then ducks below the opening until he's completely hidden. The beam of his headlamp sweeps through the treetops, then everything goes black. I catch all of this on video before hitting pause again.

"Zach?" I whisper down into the hole.

"What's taking you so long?" His voice echoes from below. "There's enough room for two down here."

I lower myself through the opening the way Zach did and feel his hands guide my feet to the ledge. He helps me down to where he's crouched on the edge of a cavern the size of a small car. I flick on my headlamp and look around at the damp, mossy limestone, then up at the opening that gapes like a mouth above our heads. The air is cool and still and smells like damp, rotting leaves. I'm seriously creeped out and don't even need to pretend when I film the next segment, but Zach is already on his knees looking for a way to climb down further.

"There's another tight spot, then it looks to open up again." He pulls his head back out of the hole and looks up at me. "You think you can squeeze through?"

"If you can, I can."

"Right then," he says and slithers his body, headfirst this time, down through a blind crack in the limestone.

Once more I follow his lead. Only I go the other way. I drop my legs into the unknown, then use my arms to lower myself through the hole. I kick my feet until I feel something solid.

"Easy! That was my head."

"Sorry!"

"About twelve inches to the left and you should feel another ledge. It's wide enough for you to crouch on but be careful. There's not as much headroom down here."

I suck in my breath and squeeze through the opening until I feel a solid mass beneath my feet. Then, again, I look around, up through the opening we just came through, and then at Zach who's crawling commando-style deeper into the crevasse. I film my face as I scrabble and squeeze after him, doing my best not to get left behind. I don't want to lose sight of his shoes even for a second.

I'm still filming when I hear his voice echo back through a low, narrow opening. "Uh, Kate? You still with me?"

There's a subdued tone to his voice that triggers the hairs on the back of my neck. Suddenly I feel chilled and my chest tightens. I shiver and swallow hard for the camera.

"Yeah, I'm right here. Can you see anything?"

"I can."

"Like what?"

"Are you still filming?"

"Yep."

"Turn it off," he says quietly.

"Why?"

"Just turn it off."

His tone is so serious, I immediately turn off the camera and push my head through the final opening.

"What's wrong?" I whisper above my pounding heart.

"Bones," he says, in his creepy, subdued tone.

That's when I see Zach stretched out on his stomach in front of me. His face is almost six feet from where I'm lying and he's face-to-face with a skull so clean and bright it looks like the moon that should have been in the night sky. Every instinct in my body screams for me to flee and I jerk my head up hard, which is when my skull collides with the solid wall of limestone above me.

"Shit!" I shout and scramble backward.

"Kate!" Zach's calm shock falls away and he starts screaming. "Get me out of here! Get me the hell out of here now!"

There's nothing to do but grab his feet and pull him backward with all my strength. It's an awkward maneuver since I'm hunched over, but it gives him the momentum he needs to push himself backward through the narrow crack and into the cavern with me. There's just enough room to sit side by side, our legs tucked up under our chins, our hearts pounding together. I feel a hot, wet patch of blood at the back of my head and hear his labored breathing. He's clearly struggling with the turn of events.

"It's okay," I say calmly. "Just breathe. We're going to be okay."

"Let's get the hell out of here. Screw your video," he says finally, then climbs roughly past me, up through the cracks and caverns toward the forest.

As much as I have zero desire to face the skull again, I push my head and shoulders back through the last opening, pull my phone from my pocket, and take a short video of the cavern and the skull staring back.

"Kate! Let's go. Now!" Zach calls out. He fumbles frantically, pulling himself up with the rope, loosening bits of dirt and limestone that rain down on me.

"Coming," I say and tuck my phone deep into my pocket for safekeeping.

When he climbs free, Zach reaches down and grabs my arms before I can even feel for the rope. I scrabble with my feet to help propel me upward, and together with Zach's unexpected strength, I manage to come through the opening of the crevasse and land in a heap on the ground beside him.

"C'mon," he says, tugging me up before I can even catch my breath. Then he drags me back through the dark forest, his headlamp shooting wildly through the trees. We trip and stumble over logs, rocks, and stumps, but we don't slow down, and I don't dare suggest any more filming. Even when we get to our bikes, we push them a few yards before jumping on and pedaling so hard, I think my lungs will burst. My calves burn and I pedal at a stand, but I still can't keep up.

"Zach!" I call out when we turn onto the main road. "Wait up."

He slows and I pull up alongside him.

"Where are we going?"

"To my house." He pants and once again shoots ahead of me,

pumping furiously. He races past my driveway and down the hill without braking, then skids into his driveway. He drops the bike on the lawn, flies across the back deck, and throws himself at the door.

"*Dad!*" he screams as he slams through the mudroom and into the kitchen.

I see an upstairs light turn on before I follow Zach inside. His father stumbles down the stairs in his boxer shorts, a look of panic gripping his face.

"What? *What?* What's going on? Are you okay?"

It's a fair question. Zach is standing in the middle of the kitchen, covered with dirt, his jeans dark with ditch water down one side. There are bits of gravel and moss in his hair and his eyes are wide with terror. His father grabs him by the shoulders and pulls him into a hug before he notices me standing in the doorway.

"I don't understand. What's wrong? Why are you up? Why are you wet? And dirty?" He looks at me. "Are you Kate?"

I nod mutely. Normally I smile and offer a handshake to my friends' parents, but the situation calls for standing silently in the shadows.

Zach's dad steps away from Zach and toward me. "Are you okay?" he asks.

I nod again, but then I reach up and touch the back of my head. When I bring my hand into the light, it's wet and sticky with blood.

"You're hurt!"

Zach's dad pulls me forward into the light.

"I'm fine," I say, although suddenly I'm not feeling fine at all. I feel like throwing up.

"Zach. Get me a wet washcloth."

Zach disappears while his dad sets me in a kitchen chair and examines my head. "You could probably use a couple of stitches."

I feel a cold pressure on the back of my head and flinch.

"Just stay still. Zach? Grab the first aid kit."

"You're not going to, like, put in stitches, are you?" I ask, alarmed, and turn in my chair to look up at him. He turns my head to face down again.

"No, I just need to clean it up, then I'll tape it closed."

I want to protest and pull free, but he's a cop, I tell myself, and I will myself to sit still.

"What happened?" he asks again.

I freeze and catch Zach's eyes from across the room. His father looks back and forth between us.

"Let's skip right to the truth."

"I hit it on a rock. Like on the side of a cave, or crevasse, or whatever."

He works on my head, snipping away bits of hair, squeezing the cut together, then taping the wound closed. He covers it with a small square of gauze. The room starts to swirl and I grab the arms of the chair for balance.

"You were in a cave? Tonight? Just the two of you?"

I don't know if it was better or worse that it was just the two of us, but I nod. Zach looks down at the wide plank flooring beneath his muddy shoes.

"Why were you in a cave? Have you been drinking?"

"No. Nothing like that," I say. "We were just exploring this cave we found on my grandfather's property." For some reason I don't feel like it's worth mentioning my YouTube channel.

"Your grandfather? Gord Cooper?" he asks as if the pieces of the puzzle don't fit together.

I shake my head. "My other grandfather. Peter Goheen."

Zach's father looks shaken at this news. "I didn't realize. I had no idea your mother and Mitch ..."

"You know my father?"

"I know *of* him. I don't know if we've ever met."

Zach starts to talk. After standing in the middle of the kitchen in total silence for what seemed like twenty minutes, he finally opens his mouth and a stream of words gush out like water from a fire hose.

"The crevasse. On the Goheen property. Way down. We had to climb down. Deep. Someone's in there. Dead. Just bones. And a skull. It was staring at me."

Zach shakes his head, as if trying to dislodge the image from his mind. His father leads him to the kitchen table and sits him down beside me. Then he goes to the fridge and grabs two cans of Coke.

"Drink these," he says. Then he leaves and comes back with two blankets that he wraps around our shoulders.

"Now. Are you sure you saw bones? A skull? Maybe your eyes played tricks on you in the dark. Maybe you just saw some sticks and a round rock?"

I pull out my phone and hand it to him. There's no mistaking it — it's a human skull, empty eye sockets and all.

Zach's father stares at the image for several minutes. He scratches his temple, then puts down the phone and rubs his face with both hands.

"What are we going to do?" Zach asks.

His father glances up at the kitchen light, then stands and paces. That's when he notices he's still in his boxer shorts, and he looks embarrassed.

"I'm going to get dressed," he says and heads up the stairs.

"I meant about the bones. The skull," Zach calls after him. But his father doesn't respond.

Zach and I don't speak. We let the enormity of our discovery sink in and listen to the hum of the refrigerator, the dripping of the kitchen tap, the thumping of his father walking overhead. I glance down at my phone. It's almost three in the morning.

"I should get home," I say suddenly. More than anything I just want to sneak back into bed without my mother ever finding out what I've done.

Zach's father reappears, dressed in jeans and a T-shirt. He pulls on a windbreaker and grabs his keys from a hook by the back door.

"I'll drop you off," he says to me.

"That's okay," I protest. "It would probably be better if I don't wake my mother."

Zach's father snorts. "It's too late for a cover story."

"Where are you going?" Zach asks.

"You and I are going to the station. I need to figure out what to do."

"What to do?" Zach says, alarmed. "You need to get over there and get that body out of the ground."

"I can't, Zach! I can't just barge onto private property without cause. And I'll need the forensics team."

"Cause? There's a dead person. Isn't that cause enough?"

"There's procedure. It has to be done right. We don't know how old the remains are. Or who they might be. We don't even know if Peter Goheen is responsible ..."

His words fade and he looks at me apologetically.

"Don't worry. I just met the guy. I don't think there's a Disney movie ending in our future," I mumble.

"But what if he realizes we're on to him? He'll move the evidence!" Zach says.

Zach is in full-blown panic mode, his eyes as wide as the old-fashioned records my mother had in our apartment out west.

"No eighty-year-old is going to climb down into a crevasse in the middle of the night and start pulling up bones," his father argues.

"He's not a normal eighty-year-old. He's like the undead. A zombie or something." Zach glances at me and looks sheepish. "No offense," he adds as an afterthought.

I shrug. "None taken. Like I said, I've only met the guy once and he wasn't exactly charming."

Zach's father throws a hoodie at Zach and waits for us to file through the door ahead of him.

"Zach, you can catch some sleep on the couch in the station's lunchroom, and Kate, I'm delivering you home."

"You can just drop me at the end of my driveway," I suggest hopefully and am surprised when he says *fine*.

✕ ✕ ✕

The sound of hammering wakes me and I look around my room, disoriented, before I recall the events of the previous night. The reentry into reality is swift and terrifying, all the more terrifying when I realize I'm not hearing hammering but someone banging on the front door.

I sneak down the top few stairs and there he is — my grand-father — standing at the door, smashing it with his fist, and screaming.

"Shit," I mutter and scamper back to my bedroom. I pull on the clothes I discarded on the floor only a few hours ago. The jeans are still damp.

Mom is yelling now too, and racing down the stairs. "Hold on. I'm coming."

I don't think she realizes who's at the door so I fly to the top of the stairs and scream down at her.

"Mom! No! Wait!"

She glances up at me but she doesn't slow down. Before I can say another word she pulls open the door. I rush down the stairs, two at a time, and come up behind her in time to see my grand-father. His eyes are wild with hatred and the loose, whiskered skin under his chin wobbles. I take a step back and reach instinc-tively for a weapon. I feel the coat rack, a sweater, Mom's purse, and then an old umbrella. I grab that and hold it in front of me protectively.

"They had no right to be nosing around my property," he yells. "Shoulda known she was yours. Off screwing around with the boys."

I feel my mother's body tense. Her shoulders creep up toward her ears. She clenches her jaw so tight I can hear her teeth grind-ing, enamel on enamel.

"Next time I see her where she's not welcome she'll be sorry."

Mom pushes me backward and steps fully into the doorway.

"Get the hell off my property!" she growls and throws her arm out toward the road, pointing violently. Her voice brims with so much rage her tone drops an octave. "You were *never* welcome here before and you certainly aren't welcome now. So get the hell away. And if you so much as look at my daughter — if you so much as glimpse her on the school bus — you won't have time to make a fist. Your bullying days are over."

The old man falters, and while he pauses to gather his words, Mom double downs on her fury, each word like a poison dart launched with precision.

"I'm not afraid of you. I'm *not*. Look at you. You're pathetic. Weak. *Powerless*. I wish Mitch could see you now."

He takes a step back, then another. Sensing his uncertainty, Mom steps onto the front porch and the screen door slams hard behind her. I step close to look out, my nose pressed against the mesh. He takes a third step back so that he's almost at the edge of the porch, about to tumble off onto the grass. And she takes another slow step forward in response, her fists tight knots at the end of her arms. I'm sure she's going to step straight up and clock him.

"Mom," I call out quietly, willing her to come back inside the house.

"Come on. Try me. I dare you. But you aren't so tough anymore, are you?" She advances with each word, gaining strength and daring as he shuffles down the porch stairs unsteadily, then back toward his pickup truck like a hermit crab, his feet scuttling along the gravel.

He reaches behind his back and opens the door to his truck, without ever taking his eyes off my mother. He spits at the ground, then climbs inside and turns on the engine. Mom lunges at him as he backs down the driveway. I'm sure she's made her point and will come back to the porch, but with so many years of pent-up anger, it's like she can't stop. She bends over and scoops up a handful of gravel, then begins hurling stones. They ping off his windshield as he reverses out to the road, his eyes never once breaking Mom's gaze.

When he's gone, Mom returns to find me standing in the hallway, still gripping the umbrella like a baseball bat. Her face is gray, and her hands are trembling.

"Who are you? Mary frigging Poppins?"

I step back to put some distance between her and me. What just happened? Who is this person standing in front of me? She crumples then. She sits down on the stairs and bursts into tears.

ZACH 5

A pickup truck is reversing fast out of Kate's driveway when we arrive. It just about collides with the front bumper of our car, pauses, then tears away. Dad slams on the brakes as its tires rip against the pavement. My body is thrown forward, then whipped back with the force of the sudden stop. Dad slams his palms against the steering wheel, barely containing a string of profanities.

I shift to an upright position again. "What the hell? Who was that?"

"Peter Goheen." Dad's tone is heavy as he pulls into the driveway.

My heart sinks hard and fast, and I rise up in my seat to get a better look at the house. Nothing is broken or looks out of place, but that doesn't mean anything. Everyone knows the worst sorts of secrets lie hidden behind the walls of a house. Dad is still putting the car in park when I swing open the car door and jump out.

"Kate? Sally?" I run toward the front porch. "Kate?" My scream echoes down the hall.

Kate steps out from the kitchen and presses open the screen door with one arm like an invitation, which I gratefully accept.

"Are you guys okay? We just saw that asshole leaving in a hurry."

Her bottom lip trembles, but she nods. "We're fine."

Sally appears behind her suddenly, floating ghostlike. Her eyelashes are damp with tears and she wipes her palms across her face.

"Mom totally kicked his ass. You should have seen it," Kate says.

My expression must give away my astonishment because Kate hurries to finish her explanation.

"Not literally. I mean, she didn't actually kick anything. But she totally put him in his place, like, with her words."

Kate scowls and some of her energy deflates as reality catches up with her.

"Six feet under would be the best place to put him," my father says.

I turn to see Dad standing behind me, an uncertain expression playing at the corners of his mouth. He nods at Kate's mom and she gestures for him to step inside. He reaches out his hand to shake.

"Al Whitchurch," he says. His voice is deeper than normal, more formal than usual. Even I can tell something's up.

"I remember you, Al," Kate's mom says lightly. She flicks a strand of hair out of her face and wipes a finger under each eye, then checks to see if she's smeared her mascara. "Long time no see."

Dad inflates slightly and pushes his shoulders back. It's a subtle change in posture, and you'd never notice if you weren't me.

"I hear you've already met my son, Zach."

Sally glances at me and nods. "Yes, I've had the pleasure. And thank you for sending him over to cut the grass."

A flash of dread washes through me, but Dad has my back. "We're happy to help. It's tough to keep on top of a property like this. So if you ever need anything ..."

"Like middle-of-the-night first aid?" Sally queries, deadpan, reaching over to touch the back of Kate's head.

Kate's eyes lock onto mine and she looks like she's begging to die.

"Would you like to sit down? It seems like we have a lot to catch up on."

Sally steps into the kitchen and my father follows. He's all gallantry and grand gestures, and if he was wearing a hat, he'd be holding it against his chest right now. Kate and I hang back and listen while her mother offers my father a muffin and a coffee. Things are getting seriously weird. And fast.

"You're still with the police force?" Sally launches into small talk.

Kate grabs my arm and drags me into the living room.

"Your mom knows everything?" I ask as panic floods my chest like a spring stream during a rainstorm.

Kate looks at the floor, then quickly up at me before she grimaces. "Not exactly *everything*."

In other words, Kate has told her mother almost nothing and in the next few minutes Sally's going to hear a lot that's going to blow her mind. I'm about to suggest we put some distance between us and the inevitable explosion, but Kate sinks onto the couch. I look around the room. It's seriously outdated with pale pink upholstery and striped wallpaper.

I drop onto the couch beside her. "You planning on redecorating ever?"

"Nah, we're both super into stinky wallpaper and dusty rose furniture. We even have a lavender bathtub upstairs."

She offers me a tight, grim smile, or maybe not really a smile at all but more an expression of resignation.

"I thought our place was special, but well, you guys get first prize. Congratulations," I say and smile for real. It's a small gesture, like getting to pick your final meal before the execution.

Kate signals for me to shut up when her mother's raised voice echoes from across the hallway.

"They what? *When?*"

My smile dissolves. "Kate. On a scale from one to ten, what's your mother's temper like?"

"Ten is bad?"

"Ten is very bad."

"Then she's, like, a twenty."

We pause and listen to the silence across the hall, which is way worse than words. At least with words you know what to expect. Silence can mean just about anything. Nothing good ever came from a simmering, silent parent. Kate grabs my wrist and squeezes.

"I'm so screwed. Especially if she finds out I was filming a video for my YouTube channel. Please tell me you didn't tell your father about *that*. And tell me some good news, quick."

My mind scrabbles around inside the dark cavern of my skull looking for something good to say. Or something funny. Or anything at all other than the fact that Kate is practically holding my hand.

"I didn't mention the video, so your secret is safe. For now. What else? Uh. Good news? Let me see. How about this? The police are on their way over to Peter Goheen's place right now with a search warrant. Dad says they'll take him into custody too. Before the day's out."

Kate lets go of my wrist and punches me in the shoulder. I think she means to be playful but the truth is, she kinda has a wicked right hook and it hurts.

"Why didn't you tell me sooner?" she says, and starts punching me faster with both hands. I try to protect myself from the blows raining down on me, but she lands one on my thigh, then on my chest. "You're such a jerk," she mutters.

"Stop, stop." I'm half laughing and half begging.

"Kate!" Sally's voice shatters our laughter and Kate freezes. I dare to look up at Dad and Sally standing shoulder to shoulder in the doorway. Dad looks resigned, but the level-twenty temper straining Sally's face makes me glad I get to leave with Dad.

I glance quickly at Kate, who has assumed an appropriately remorseful face. But Sally isn't a pushover. She places her hands on her hips with perfect symmetry and lowers her gaze.

"Zach is spending the day with us so go upstairs and put on some clean clothes."

Kate doesn't dare make eye contact with me, but she stands up obediently and takes a tentative step toward the door. When Dad and Sally move to let her through, Kate pauses. "Where are we going?"

"Somewhere you and Zach can't sneak back to Peter Goheen's," my father says sternly, in a tone that sounds so uncharacteristic it's almost theatrical, like he and Sally planned the whole scene, right down to the dialogue.

"That's not fair!" I blurt. "We found the ..." I falter, "... evidence."

Dad snorts. "Sorry, Zach. You've been reassigned to desk duty."

"What about school?" I ask.

"It's your lucky day. I already called the attendance line saying you're staying home."

Kate's shoulders slump as she rounds the corner into the hall. I hear her climbing the stairs, slowly, one step at a time like she's walking to her death. I collapse back in the couch and start counting all the reasons I'm pissed. As for Dad and Sally, well, without another word they return to the kitchen to finish their coffees and catch up. Life can be seriously exasperating when you're a teenager.

✕ ✕ ✕

Sally drags Kate and me all the way to the city to a restaurant supply outlet to buy silverware for her new restaurant. After the silverware, we buy dinner plates. And dessert plates. And soup bowls. And coffee cups. Wine glasses. Salt and pepper shakers. Bread baskets. Frying pans. Stock pots. Slotted spoons. Tongs. Spatulas.

The place is ginormous, thousands of square feet. Rows and rows. It's tortuous. If they'd spent two weeks devising ways to punish me, they couldn't have come up with a better plan.

"Plain is better than patterned. Adds style."

"Square is too trendy. You'll regret getting those. Round is classier."

"Silverware should have a good weight to it, and an interesting design. What do you think, Zach?"

I nod absently. I had no idea anyone could have opinions on such things.

"I'm going to wait outside," I say finally when Sally turns down the linen aisle. There's no way I can listen to an hour on the merits of white versus colored napkins.

I step outside into the bright sunshine and look left, then right. The restaurant supply store is in a strip mall in the middle of a business park. In the same complex there are stores selling vacuum cleaners, discount patio furniture, automotive supplies, paint, and yarn. I glance back through the window at Kate, who is pushing an overflowing cart behind Sally. The set of her shoulders tells me we aren't going home anytime soon.

I sit on the curb and take out my phone.

There's a text from Josh: *You okay? Not on the bus and not in class?*

I start to text, then delete. What exactly should I tell Josh? After three more attempts, I finally text: *I'm fine. Long story. Talk later?*

He shoots me a thumbs-up, which means he's not paying attention to whatever's going on in English.

I glance back through the expanse of glass but Sally and Kate are nowhere to be seen, still lost somewhere among an acre of aisles.

✗ ✗ ✗

When we finally get back to Kate's house and finish helping Sally unload the boxes, Kate takes my hand and drags me upstairs to her bedroom. She pulls me inside and closes the door.

I glance at the closed door and then at her.

"Your mom's cool with this?"

"God, no. Not usually. Whenever Austin was over, I had to have the door wide open and we had to be on the side of the room she could see from the couch. No sneaking into the corner."

"Austin?" I ask.

"Just someone I used to know," she says with an eye roll. "I thought he was cool. But I was wrong." She reaches up to feel the back of her head.

I choose not to pursue the topic of Austin and say instead: "Does it hurt?"

"Not too much. I just forgot it was there."

I'm still standing in the center of the room, not sure whether to open the door or go with it. I have no interest in testing Sally's level-twenty temper twice in one day.

"Don't worry. I bought us some brownie points with all that shopping. Besides, she'll be busy unpacking that shit for hours. And as bad as this room is, the other rooms are worse."

My heart is freaking out a little and I feel suddenly made up of angles and dissecting lines. I don't know where to put my hands or how to hold my arms, and I'm aware of standing stiff and straight like some sort of robot. The only thing that moves is my blood and my rabbiting heart. Kate is surely used to someone smoother than me, someone, maybe even Austin, who knows a few moves or has a couple of good lines to ease the tension. But I stand there like an idiot feeling acutely aware of how skinny my legs are, how knotted my knees. I worry that a panic attack is going to hit, but Kate comes to the rescue and smiles. She gestures up at an old poster from some eighties music magazine and says: "Zach, I'd like you to meet my friend, David Bowie. David, this is Zach Whitchurch." She films the introduction.

I can't help but laugh and look around her room more closely.

"Seriously, Kate. What's up with this?"

Kate grimaces. "I decided to go retro with my decorating scheme. You don't like it?"

With the ice broken, my limbs become flexible again and I'm able to breathe. My heart slows to its normal rhythm and the tightness in my chest loosens. I continue to look around and it kind of blows my mind. I mean, there's a bulletin board on the wall that has concert ticket stubs from the seventies and eighties. I step closer to read the bands: The Who. Rush. Queen. Teenage Head. Sally must have been a bit wild in her day.

"This was your mom's room?"

Kate nods.

"Weird that it's all still here. Like she never moved away."

"Tell me about it."

A vehicle pulls up outside and I glance out the window in time to see Dad put the car in park and step out. He stretches his back like he does after a long day, then ducks back inside to grab something. Before he shuts the door, he checks his hair in the side mirror. I mean, he actually really does that and I have so much secondhand embarrassment my cheeks flush hot.

"Did your dad just check himself out?" Kate squeals.

My stomach turns heavy with dread when I turn to see her covering her laughter with her hands. "Oh. My. God. Your dad is *totally* into my mom."

The heat returns to my cheeks but Kate pushes my shoulder and distracts me.

"Wait? You already knew?! Did he tell you?"

I shake my head and glance at David for some bro support.

"Hey, don't be embarrassed. It happens all the time. Do you know how many of my teachers have hit on my mom? And my soccer coaches?"

I shake my head again and wish I could think of one, just one, witty sarcastic comment to make.

"Don't worry. She lets them down easy. Your dad won't feel a thing."

We hear Sally greet my father and invite him inside. The screen door slams shut and I imagine him standing in the front hall, at the base of the stairs, trying to bring his A game for Sally Cooper.

"Kate! Zach!" Sally calls up. "Zach! Your dad's here."

Kate's eyes flash with glee and she throws open the bedroom door.

"Coming!" she yells down before she turns to me and says: "Let the games begin!"

By the time we get downstairs, Sally has my dad seated at the table and is offering him a plate of pumpkin tarts. His eyes flicker between her face and the plate.

"Lemonade?" Sally asks him.

He nods and I feel my cheeks flush hot again. Kate knocks her shoulder against mine, quickly, without our parents noticing, and I'm almost grateful for the distraction.

Dad takes a tart and a bite, then notices me standing in the room. He kicks out a chair and nods for us to take a seat.

"Did you find the skull?" Kate asks with a bit more enthusiasm than is appropriate considering someone is dead.

Dad swallows his bite of tart then washes it down with a gulp of lemonade. He stops and looks at the glass.

"Lavender," Sally says.

"It's good," he says with both surprise and approval.

Kate and I watch Sally's face and I definitely see a flicker of something significant. Appreciation? Happiness? Amusement?

"Yes," Dad continues. "We found the skull. Right where you described. We also found the remains of a second individual."

He looks directly at Sally and suddenly the room changes. The mood darkens. The summery brightness washing in through the window cools. What had seconds ago felt like a friendly conversation punctuated with flirting glances suddenly feels overly still and somber.

"What?" Kate and I say at the same time. We exchange glances, trying to figure out what's going on.

But when I look at Sally, I see something more like shock in her expression. The color has drained from her face. She's trembling.

Kate catches the look too and seems to understand something serious is happening. Her tone goes from smart-ass teenager to deep, terrified concern. "What's going on? Mom?"

Sally looks at Kate but doesn't speak. She looks at my dad and he doesn't speak either, but the corners of his mouth pull back with grim resignation.

"I'm sorry to do this now. I'm hoping I can collect a sample of DNA," he says finally, with so much compassion my ears start to whine like a concrete drill. "But I can come back in a bit. After you've had a chance to process all this and talk with your, uh, daughter."

KATE 5

Zach and his dad leave Mom and I sitting at the kitchen table. They let themselves out quietly but still we jump when the screen door closes. We're both clearly on edge, and because I'm not sure what's coming, I sit as silently as the skull in the cave and wonder what it has to do with my mother.

Finally, Mom sighs three decades of pent-up emotion. She starts to talk without looking at me, examining her hands instead, picking at the cuticle around her left thumb.

"I don't know if I've ever told you about my brother, James."

"You have a brother?" I ask, incredulous, trying to piece together the reasons I might never have heard of him.

She nods and continues to stare down at her hands that are now nested in her lap.

"Where is he?" I ask.

"I don't know."

"What do you mean, you don't know? Did he disappear?" My tone makes it sound impossible, like people don't just up and disappear one day. But when she looks up, her face is altered. She's aged ten years in a few, brief seconds. Our eyes meet and I shiver. It's spooky.

"Yes. He did. In 1982, when he was fifteen."

She starts to cry slowly, like a storm that gives a few warning drips before the winds pick up. Then before I know it, she's crying big, fat tears that streak her face and fall off her jaw. I'm not used to my mother crying. She's too tough to cry. But her tears temper my anger and a protective calm washes over me.

"Did you call the police?"

Mom nods and wipes away the tears with her palms.

"Of course we called the police. They searched everywhere. But he was just ... gone. I'm sorry. This is such a shock. After all these years."

"Wait. You guys think the bones ... In the cave ... You think maybe it's him?"

Mom sniffles and looks at me apologetically. My mind races to assemble the pieces of the day's events, and the events that took place long before I came along. Then my brain pulls together one huge idea and flashes it like a marquee though my mind: that skull might have been ... my uncle?

Suddenly the thought of editing and posting my video seems insensitive and cruel. In fact, all of my urbex videos come into a new focus. What if people recognized the abandoned houses we'd filmed? What if I've highlighted bad memories, or trampled good memories? My heart sinks low in my chest and pumps a slow, sad rhythm.

"Then who's the other ... person ... they found?" I ask.

"His friend. Luke. Luke McLeod."

"They both went missing?"

She nods.

"At the same time?"

She nods again.

"How old were you? When he went missing."

"Seventeen." She takes a deep breath, then slumps in her chair, and the essence of my mother drains out until I can barely recognize her.

"What was he like? Do you have a picture of him?"

She shakes her head sadly. "I wish. My mother took them all down. Dad wouldn't let us talk about him so there was no way we were going to have a picture of him hanging on the wall."

That's when I remember the photo in my backpack — the one of my mother as a graduate. There had been a second photo tucked in that frame but I didn't have a chance to look before the bus arrived, then I forgot all about it. I jump up and grab my backpack from the hall.

The second photo is older, a black-and-white picture of two shaggy-haired kids standing in front of an old farmhouse. I look closer. It's the same house we're living in now. In the photo, both kids are in cutoff jeans and bare feet. The older kid, my mother, is wearing a plaid, western-style shirt with the tails tied above her waist. She stands about a foot taller than a boy who's wearing a Star Wars T-shirt and has a Frisbee in his hand, hanging beside his thigh. She looks to be about fifteen or sixteen — about my age. He's a couple of years younger. There's a long, square, old-fashioned car in the distance, beyond the house, and a dog sitting beside the boy's feet.

I hand the photo to my mother.

"Is that him?"

She takes a quick look at the photo then clutches it to her chest. When she can stand to look again, she peels it away from her body slowly, as if she's savoring the moment. Then she stares at the photo and starts crying again. I lean over, put my hand on her back, and give a little rub. I don't think I've touched her like this in years.

"It was hidden behind your graduation photo. The one that fell off the wall," I offer.

She looks up at me and I see the expression in her eyes shift from sorrow to hope. She takes a decisive swipe at her cheeks and stands up.

"Maybe there are others?" she says and darts across the hall into the living room. She looks around wildly at the photos hung on the walls and perched on end tables.

"Dad wouldn't let anyone talk about James after he disappeared. He said that chapter of our lives was finished. It was like he wanted to forget James even existed. They always had a tense relationship. I mean, my father was a miserable drunk. But after that night, he made my mother erase James from the house. I hated her for that. It was bad enough she didn't stick up for James when he was alive, but when he disappeared, she still let Dad control him. It's part of the reason I left home."

She takes all the photos from the walls and starts to disassemble them. Behind a photo of my grandparents on their twenty-fifth wedding anniversary is a school portrait of James.

"He's twelve in this one. I remember that stupid hockey jersey. It was practically falling to pieces but he insisted on wearing it for picture day. Mom was so embarrassed. Especially when he ended up in the front row for the class photo."

She stares at the picture like it's a long-lost friend and a tender smile plays with the corners of her mouth.

"He was such a stubborn kid. Man, he drove me crazy. But he could be so sweet too. He used to sneak into my room to sleep when I was out late. Just to make sure I got home safe. He was always looking out for me. And he was two years younger."

She hands me a stack of photo frames.

"Here. Help me open these."

By the time we finish opening every frame in the living room, we have seventeen photos of James and it's like Mom just won the lottery. There are baby photos and photos from when he was a preschooler. There are photos of him on sports teams and one of him driving a tractor. One frame has three photos, piled like refugees behind a photo of me and Mom overlooking the ocean. The last in the stack is of Mom, my father, James, plus another guy with dark curly hair and ridiculous round sunglasses. They're standing by a farm gate with beer cans lined along the top. James is holding a long narrow gun at his side, pointing it at the ground, and grinning wide.

"Who's this?" I ask, pointing to the only dude in the world who missed the memo that flared pant legs were out of fashion in the eighties.

"That was a friend of your father's from the city." She stops and thinks for a moment. "Todd? Tom? Tony, maybe? Yeah, I think it was Tony. He used to come up sometimes for the week-ends and hang out. James idolized him and my girlfriend, Jenn, had a major crush on him. I forgot all about him. No idea where he is now."

In the end, I don't have the heart to ask about how James dis-appeared or the other million questions zapping around inside my brain like a lightning storm. I know there's time for that. Instead, I listen to her reminisce about a brother she finally has permis-sion to remember. That's when I realize that even though I've been missing my friends on the west coast, it's nothing compared to how much Mom has silently missed James all these years. Suddenly, we have more in common than I ever thought possible.

✖ ✖ ✖

When Zach's father returns a couple of hours later, he's alone. He knocks softly on the wooden frame of the screen door and Mom hoists herself up with so much effort you'd think she had a three-hundred-pound weight strapped to her. When he sees me standing behind Mom, he says, "Sorry, Kate. Zach's at home. He had homework."

I'm embarrassed he thinks I came to the door hoping to see Zach, and I stutter my way through an explanation. "Yeah. No worries. I wasn't really expecting him. I just … you know. Came to support Mom."

He takes out a long swab and asks Mom to open her mouth.

"It's just a formality, really," he says quietly while he swipes it across the inside of her cheeks and screws it into a plastic vial. "There was plenty of evidence to ID them."

"Like what?" I ask when Mom falters.

"The remnants of old blue jeans, with a container of Tic Tacs in the pocket. Adidas running shoes. A leather belt. And a wallet. With James's student ID card in it."

Mom gasps. She covers her mouth with both hands like she's worried about having to catch her lunch coming back up.

"James and his Tic Tacs. I don't know whether to laugh or cry," she says before her chest heaves with a massive, tsunami-like sob.

"The police are contacting Mr. McLeod now for his DNA sample. We should have results in a few days. Then we'll know for sure."

✗ ✗ ✗

That night, as I'm settling in and replaying the events of the day, my phone vibrates. I pick it up to see Zach sent a text.

U there?

Yep

Did you post your video?

Nah. Doesn't seem like the right thing to do. You know?

I know. So whatcha doing?

Nothing. Scrolling through Instagram to see what my friends out west are doing. It's mostly the truth.

Missing anything good?

Beach party. Bonfire, I text, even though I'm not sure I'd be invited even if I was there.

Bummer.

It's okay. I can party anytime. Not every day you find your dead uncle you didn't even know existed.

We did good I guess.

I guess so. Just a minute. Be right back!

I sneak downstairs and take a picture of the photo of Mom and James standing in front of the house. Then I send it to Zach and sneak back upstairs.

Is that a picture of your uncle?

Your dad told you?

Yep.

We found a bunch. This is my favorite.

See you tomorrow on the bus? Zach texts.

Yep, I text back.

Want me to save you a seat?

Absolutely.

ZACH 6

The first thing Kate does when she sits down beside me on the bus the next day is hand me a photo of James, an eight-by-ten-inch portrait. He looks very young, still has his baby teeth and a shy, eager smile.

"Cute. Where did you find it?"

"They were hidden behind all the old family photos in the living room."

She hands me another from when he's a bit older and I hold it up to her face.

"He has the same eyes but your hair is completely different."

Kate rolls her eyes. "Yep. I got the Cooper hair. He must have got his from my grandmother's side. It's so straight." Kate holds the picture and examines it. "He has a nice smile though. He looks sweet."

"He looks like a troublemaker if you ask me."

"Why? Because of the long hair?" She raises her eyebrows at me and I raise my hand to feel my own hair, hanging long around my face.

"No," I say defensively. "It's more like his expression. I dunno. It's like he's been caught doing something bad."

"If you look close enough, he has a dimple." She touches the photo. "And a bit of a cowlick." Her voice is soft and nostalgic and takes me by surprise.

I have dimples, I think to myself, but instead I say, "I wonder what Luke looked like?"

Kate cocks her head. "I dunno. Maybe there's something online."

"Let's see what we can find over lunch," I suggest as the bus pulls up to the school. "I have another idea too. Meet me at the bleachers at noon."

When the bus doors groan open, I jump off and head straight to the library. Mrs. Hudson, the librarian, glances up. Twice. First, she looks up when I open the door and then she does a double take when she sees it's me. To be fair, I haven't been in the library for a while. She scowls and gives me that *what are you doing here?* look. I smile apologetically and head for where she keeps the old school yearbooks. If you can believe it, there's one for every year dating back to 1968. But I can tell by the layer of dust on the books that nobody has picked them up in a long time, at least not the ones that go back as far as the 1970s and '80s.

I pick out a couple of books near what I figure was my father's graduation year, sit on the floor, and start flipping through. The first photo I find of Dad shows him standing in the second row of the football team. Except for his super nerdy haircut, he looks good in his uniform, and really young.

Next, I flip to the grade nine photos and find Sally Cooper. She looks like a shampoo model with long hair and a big smile filled with perfectly aligned teeth. It's obvious Sally and Kate look a lot alike. Next, I select more recent years, hoping to find a photo of James Cooper. I finally find him listed in the 1981 yearbook twice. There's his class picture, then a candid of him in the small engine shop leaning over a lawn mower.

x x x

Later, when the lunch bell finally sounds, I jump from my seat and practically sprint to the bleachers. By the time Kate shows up, I'm deep into my phone and halfway through my sandwich. I try not to notice her approach. I mean, it never helps to look too eager, right?

"Hey," she says when she climbs to my row and sets down her backpack.

"Hey!" I say and pause long enough to take a bite of my sandwich.

She takes out a square plastic box and opens the lid to reveal a row of sushi rolls, takes one with her fingers, and pops it in her mouth.

She chews as she leans over to see what I'm doing. "There's Wi-Fi out here?"

I nod.

"Did you find anything?" she asks.

"Check out this cold case website."

I show her my phone and she types in the address, then scrolls through until we find photos of both James and Luke. It shows them at the age they disappeared and then with age-progression photos showing how they would have looked at twenty-five. There's nothing more recent. Nothing to show what fifty-year-old James and Luke might look like.

"There're actually a few cold case forums that have streams on James and Luke. And it looks like there might be some newspaper articles," I say. Then I toss the yearbook on the bench. "Check out the index. James is listed twice."

Kate flips through and looks at the photos.

"That's definitely the same kid in the photo with my mom. Where'd you find this, anyway?"

"Library."

"Can I have it?"

"Sure. It'll probably be years before Mrs. Hudson realizes it's missing."

"Did your dad go to school here? With my mom?" Kate asks as she flips through the pages of old black-and-white photos looking for her mother.

"I think they were in school together one year. Did you know your mom won the Athletic Prize in grade nine?"

Kate's mouth gapes open. "No? Really? Seriously? She's never been interested in sports."

I watch my phone and wait for an old article to load. When it finally does, I see it's part of a series about local cold cases and was written on the tenth anniversary of the boys' disappearance. Kate leans close so we can read it together. Her hair brushes my face and I drink in the smell of vanilla.

John McLeod meets me at a local coffee shop. It's been ten years since his son Luke vanished without a trace on August 26, 1982. His hand shakes as he sips his coffee but he's determined to tell me the story because he still believes someone knows what happened that night. He has never stopped trying to make the facts public in case it jogs someone's memory. He reminds me that it might take only one small clue to break the case finally.

"We'd just moved to the area that summer," Mr. McLeod explains. "We'd come from down south so everything was new to us. Our place was out on Valley Road, not too far from the gravel pit. There weren't many houses nearby but Luke was an outgoing kid and he'd made friends with James Cooper who lived one farm over. James was fifteen, like Luke, and they had a lot of common interests, like muscle cars and video games.

"Wait!" I say. "Luke lived next door to James. One farm over." My heart is doing these crazy flips like it wants to squirm right out of my chest. Kate waits to see where I'm going with my revelation. "*We* live one farm over from *you*."

She pauses, then shivers and says, "That's seriously creepy." I tilt my phone back toward her face.

"It was one of those warm summer nights in August and Luke said he was going to ride over to James's place to see what he was doing. Because we were new to the area, we didn't know it at the time, but Gord Cooper had a reputation for being an abusive drunk. Our first night in our new place in fact, there were two police cars and an ambulance at the Coopers' place. I remember saying at the time somebody must have been murdered. My wife told me I was being ridiculous. We found out later he'd been on a bender and sent James to the hospital with broken ribs.

"Anyway, Luke rode off and that's the last I saw of him. When he didn't come home, I phoned over to the Coopers'. This was maybe eleven o'clock. Mrs. Cooper answered and said she hadn't seen the boys all evening.

We went out looking for them, but it was hopelessly dark by then. So we waited until morning to search again. There still wasn't a trace of them so we called the police.

"The police officer told us not to worry. They said boys that age sometimes disappeared for a day or two. When I told them Luke would never disappear like that, he tried to brush me off. But when I mentioned James Cooper, his attitude changed completely. He put out a bulletin on the boys immediately. That's when they were officially considered missing, although it had been almost eighteen hours by then. And that's when all hell broke loose. I think they had every cop in a five-hundred-mile radius on the Cooper farm. They turned that place upside down but never found a thing."

Kate stops reading and holds her last sushi roll in front of her mouth. "It sounds like my grandfather was a suspect. But why would he want to kill two boys?"

I shrug. "Not just why, but *how* would he kill two fifteen-year-old boys? I mean, I'm fifteen. How could you kill two of me?"

"With a gun?" she says and starts to chew.

"Okay, but then it comes back to *why?*"

Kate swallows her last bite. "Maybe he shot one by accident and then he had no choice but to shoot the other?"

"Then what? He cleans the gun and hides two bodies in a crevasse before anyone notices and the police show up?"

"Maybe there was more than one person."

"Let's suppose it was your grandfather, like Mr. McLeod seems to be implying. Who's going to help a violent drunk cover up two murders?"

"I dunno. Maybe you help *because* he's a violent drunk. And you're afraid of him. Like my grandmother was probably afraid of him. I know my mother was."

We turn back to continue reading but that's where the first article ends. There are three more in the series, but before we can start into number two, the bell rings. So we pack up our things and head to our afternoon classes.

KATE 6

When I get home from school after my fourth day at Hicksville High, Mom is upstairs in the far front bedroom searching through every drawer and examining every piece of paper she can find. She has the closet wide open and boxes spill across the bed.

"Whatcha doing?" I ask from the doorway.

Mom looks up and wipes the hair off her sweaty face. She's wearing shorts and a tank top. It's another hot day and the second floor of the century-old farmhouse is like a sauna.

"I'm looking to see if Mom stashed anything else of James's. If she saved those photos, she might have hidden other things from my father. I doubt he would have looked in here himself."

"Why not?"

"This was James's room. I don't think he ever stepped foot in here after he made Mom redecorate."

"How awful *was* your dad?" I dare to ask.

Mom sinks onto the corner of the bed and sighs. She must have guessed I was going to start asking questions. Maybe that's why she didn't tell me about James in the first place.

"When he was sober he was fine. He was actually pretty funny. Kind almost. But when he drank, he was a completely different man. Doctor Jekyll and Mr. Hyde."

"Did he ever hurt you?"

"Not physically. James got the brunt of that for some reason. But he was cruel to me and Mom, like emotionally. There's a reason why I moved as far away as I could."

I step across the room and open the window to let in some fresh air, then I start sorting through a box on the bed.

"Have you looked through all of these?"

"Not yet. I was still digging them out of the closet. Mom was such a hoarder!"

"Did Mitch ... my dad ... know Grandpa?"

"Sure, they met when Mitch was over. Like when he'd come by to pick me up and take me out. But honestly, most people stayed clear of him. You never knew when he was going to tie one on."

"Why didn't Grandma leave him? Why did she put up with him for so long? I mean, it must have been lonely living here with him all those years."

Mom looks up at the ceiling as if it might give her an answer. But in the end she just shrugs.

"That's the million-dollar question, isn't it? I know Aunt Kathy and Uncle Darren begged her to leave him when they moved away. I begged her to leave too, many times. I asked her to move out west with us. But she wouldn't hear of it. She could barely leave him for a weekend. I think she only ever went away one or two times without him in her whole life. Like down to visit her brother in Tennessee after we lost James. I guess being here meant she could hold on to James somehow, or what was left of him at least."

"So you guys figured he was dead?"

Mom doesn't answer right away and I wonder if she's afraid to admit it, as if saying it out loud would make it too real.

"A year after he went missing there was a memorial for both boys. I think everyone assumed by then they were dead. The technical term was *presumed dead*. The town council dedicated a bench and a tree in the park uptown. But the McLeods had moved away by then."

She rummages through the closet while I sort through the boxes on the bed. Mostly they're filled with old letters and greeting cards. One box has a bundle of newspaper clippings and recipes clipped from magazines. But at the bottom of another is an old Adidas shoebox tied neatly with ribbon, like a present.

"Did you see this?"

When I hand it to her, she sits down and unties the ribbon carefully. There's a slowness to her movements that makes me think either she's afraid of what she might find or she wants to savor the anticipation.

"Oh my God!" She covers her mouth with her hands and the box almost slips off her knees.

Inside are the kind of mementos every mother keeps as her child grows: locks of golden hair, a jewelry box full of baby teeth, report cards, hand-drawn Mother's Day cards, pieces of art that get progressively better from one year to the next. I pick up a pencil-crayon drawing of an old car.

"He drew this?"

"He adored cars." Mom takes it and flips it over. "Mom dated everything. Look. He was twelve when he drew this. It was his dream car."

"What is it?"

"A Dodge Charger. It was from a TV show we used to watch."

I pull a yellowed piece of construction paper from the box. It's another hand drawing, but from a much earlier time, with scrawled printing along the bottom that says: *James and Grover*.

"Who was Grover?"

"A blue monster from *Sesame Street*."

Although the figures are a bit primitive looking, neither is a blue monster.

"No kidding. Was there another Grover?"

I hand the drawing to Mom.

"Oh, dear. I forgot about *that* Grover. It was his imaginary friend when he was about six or seven. For months all we heard about was *Grover Carter* and all the fun things they did together. If James got a treat, Grover had to have one too. Mom thought it was adorable. I was so jealous of Grover. I think James actually liked him better than me."

Mom laughs and shakes her head, then lays the drawing carefully on the bed.

"Grover Carter? He gave his imaginary friend a last name?"

"Carter is actually James's middle name. James Carter Cooper."

I stare at Grover and James while Mom continues to pick bits and pieces from the box.

"There's his grade eight graduation certificate." Mom pulls it from the box and turns it over in case something is written on the back, but there's nothing. Below is another certificate.

"Small engine award?" I ask.

"He got the top marks in his grade nine small engine class. He loved tearing engines apart even when he wasn't in school."

At the very bottom of the box there's an old cassette tape, the kind they had when my mom was a kid and you could record your own songs, or even your voice. It's labeled *Rock 'n Roll Hour with DJ James.* The songs are written in pen on the front cover in two rows: Side A and Side B. Mom leans over to see what I'm looking at.

"He made that from my record collection, one night ..." She pauses to search for the right words, then finishes quietly. "A few weeks before he disappeared."

"Those old records you had in the apartment out west? The ones you put in storage ... until we go back?"

Mom smiles and nods, but it's a heavy smile, not one filled with joy. "Whenever I went out with my friends at night, I let him hang out in my room so he could make mixed tapes and play them on his boom box."

When Mom finishes sorting through to the bottom of the shoebox, she replaces everything, including the cassette, and sets it on the bed. Then she stands up and stretches.

"I've been up here for hours. It's time to take a break. Do you want to go into town for dinner?"

I grab the cassette when she turns her head and tuck it in my back pocket.

"Yeah. I'm starving. Let's go," I say and follow her from the room.

I've always liked driving with Mom. It means I can ask her the questions I wouldn't normally ask. There's built-in safety because I don't have to look at her face and, more importantly, she can't look at mine. So I welcome the chance to sit in the car with her for twenty minutes while we drive into town.

On the way past Zach's place, I turn in my seat to see if he's outside. But the yard is empty and I wonder what he's doing. I remember our conversation on the bleachers at lunch.

"Hey Mom? Were they very big guys?"

I want to be sensitive to my mother's feelings but I can't shake the idea that it would be basically impossible to kidnap two teenage boys.

"I dunno. James was small for his age and pretty lightweight. But Luke was maybe five foot eight. He looked pretty strong."

"Where were they last seen?"

Mom drums the steering wheel with her fingers and checks the rearview mirror even though ours is the only car on the road.

"Behind my girlfriend's house. They dropped me off in the field car so I could spend the night. Then they drove back toward Aunt Kathy's."

"But they never made it?"

"No. We found the car parked near the gravel pit the next day but there wasn't a trace of James or Luke."

"So you were the last person to see them?"

There's a chasm of silence. "Yes."

"And how were they? Were either of them acting weird?"

"I'd never actually met Luke before so I wouldn't know. But James, well, he was just being his regular self. A little bit hyper. He had a run-in with Dad earlier. I wasn't with them very long and we were driving in that old beater so it wasn't like we had much of a conversation."

She hesitates, like she has more she wants to say. But she stays silent. She checks her rearview mirror for the fiftieth time and stops at a set of lights.

"I guess the police probably questioned you about being the last person to see them."

She exhales. "They did. It felt like hours. For a while I thought they suspected me. Maybe that's why I always blamed myself for letting them drive off. I've always felt like if I'd done something even a little bit different, things would have turned out better."

"I'm sure there was nothing you could have done."

"That's what everyone told me. But I could never shake the feeling, like I was somehow responsible." Mom seems to fade into the background like a chameleon, taking on the color and texture of the tan car seats.

We're on the outskirts of town and I take a video out the window. Even though it's a small community, I haven't seen every neighborhood and even this morning on the bus I noticed a new shoe store. We drive past the high school where a few students are hanging outside. It looks like they've just returned from a school trip.

"So, what do you think happened?" I ask finally.

Mom shakes her head. "Another million-dollar question. I know most people assumed my father was involved. But I don't know how he could have been."

"What did Grandma think?"

"We never talked about it. For the first few days the place was crawling with police officers and we never had a moment alone. We barely left the house. When that died down, my father made her pack up James's room. And that was that."

Mom pulls the car into a parking lot and shuts off the engine. She looks over at me and offers up an apologetic little smile.

"Let's go eat. Okay? I know you're curious, but maybe it's better to leave this one to the police to solve."

Mom chooses a diner that has apparently been operating since she was a kid and still makes old-fashioned milkshakes. It looks like the décor hasn't changed in the years since.

"This is where all the cool kids hung out when I was a teen-ager," she says as we push through the glass door.

"So, what you're telling me is that you've never eaten here," I counter without missing a beat.

She swats me on the shoulder, but laughs one of her deep-belly laughs, the kind that takes us both by surprise. It feels good to have a bright, hard moment of happiness between us.

ZACH 7

Kate is coming down the track toward me when she stops and checks her phone, then puts it to her ear. She talks for five of the longest minutes of my life before she puts it in her back pocket and continues walking. As she climbs the bleachers, she watches me watching her. And she doesn't flinch. She doesn't look away like most people would to examine her feet or glance up at the sky. Instead, she smiles. Her confidence lights up the day like a second sun. Like an idiot, I glance down at my phone without smiling back.

She drops her bag on the seat beside me and I think she might say something about whoever she was talking to, but nope.

"What's for lunch?" she asks, glancing at my brown paper bag.

"I'm afraid to look, actually. When I bragged about your mom making you sushi, Dad offered to make me something special."

"Can he cook?"

"To answer that we'd have to deconstruct our versions of what it means to *cook*."

She raises her eyebrows. "For someone who likes to ditch school, you use a lot of academic-sounding words."

When Kate opens her lunch, I lean over and see a gourmet-looking pesto pasta salad with cherry tomatoes and black olives that makes my stomach grumble. On the other hand, I have …

"What *is* that?" Kate glances over and covers her nose with her hand. "It reeks."

I hold up a cracker with a sardine on top. There's a strip of spinach wrapped around the middle. Although there's no head, it's pretty disturbing to see the hollowed-out body lying there, soaking into the cracker. I show Kate the plastic container. Inside are four more sardine crackers.

"That's seriously disgusting." She looks like she's going to lose her breakfast. "What's *wrong* with your father?"

"He's a bit of a smart-ass."

"Is it even edible?"

"Probably, if you're a cat."

"Do you have a cat?"

I shake my head.

"So that's your dad's idea of sushi, huh? Twisted." Kate hands me a container of carrot sticks and ranch dip. "Mom always packs more than I can eat."

I nibble carrots and scan my phone.

"What're you reading?"

"Part four of that series from yesterday."

I shift close beside her and we continue reading together.

After ten years, John McLeod is no closer to the truth. "I thought the $25,000 reward would bring someone forward, but it's done no good. I hate to admit it, but Luke must be dead. If he was alive, he'd contact his mother and me. I know he would. Without a body though, my heart refuses to give up. Everybody tells me to move on, but that's impossible when it's your kid. You don't give up on your kid until there's closure of some kind.

"As much as I want to blame Gord Cooper, there are days when it just doesn't sit with me. The drunker he got, the worse he got, but think about that. A drunk doesn't do anything well and yet Luke and James disappeared without a trace."

John McLeod pauses and looks tired. I ask him if he can think of anyone who might have helped Gord Cooper cover up a crime.

"There was a neighbor on the second concession he was pretty tight with who was a nasty piece of work. He was the kind of guy everyone had a story about. And not a good story either. I won't mention his name because he'll sue me if I do. But his alibi checked out and there was no motive."

Kate turns to me. "Peter Goheen."
I nod solemnly. Then turn back to the article on my phone.

"There were conflicting theories, of course, and all tied to conflicting evidence. It's hard to sort out the truth. Some say the boys were buried on the Cooper property and that Gord Cooper's boots were covered in red clay the next day which proves he's guilty. That red clay intrigued me for the longest time but he said he spent the day fixing the cattle trough at the back of his place and there's all sorts of red clay back there.

"So that leaves us with the theory that the boys ran away. But they didn't take their bikes. Luke's was still leaning against a tree at James's aunt's house and James's bike was at home in the garage. I'm not even sure how Luke's bike ended up there to tell you the truth. The farm car they were driving was found near the gravel pit.

"Some people thought they went swimming and drowned. But the police brought in divers to search the quarry. No bodies. And if they hitchhiked somewhere, wouldn't someone have seen them? And why didn't they come back?"

Now the tears John McLeod has been holding back for an hour come rolling down his cheeks.

"It's been a long ten years. Not a day goes by I don't think about Luke. I really need to know what happened to my son."

"Omigod, that's so sad." Kate wipes at her eyes.

I know she's thinking about her mother.

× × ×

I'm lying on the couch watching Netflix after school when Dad yells from the front door.

"Zach? Can you give me a hand?"

I press pause and go find out what he needs. Normally he asks for help bringing in the groceries or carrying something like lumber or lawn furniture that takes two people. This time he needs help lugging about thirty boxes into the dining room, a space we haven't used since Mom left.

"Just stack them in the corner, by number," he says.

"What are these?" I ask as I drop a box onto the floor with a thud. A cloud of dust rises into the air and particles hang in the beam of evening sun slanting through the dining room window.

"Cold case files. Cooper and McLeod."

My heart does a little flip. I mean, it's not out of the realm of normal for Dad to bring home case files, whether he's technically allowed to or not. Bringing work home was always a point of tension with Mom, but now I guess he's given up. He sees me eyeing the boxes we've already dragged inside.

"If I have to stay at work to review all this stuff, I'll never get home."

"You're reopening the case," I say matter-of-factly. It's not a question. I sneeze and send the dust particles swirling again. Dad sizes up the room but doesn't suggest we clean it.

"I'm hungry. Let's go into town. What do you feel like eating?" Dad asks after all the boxes are stacked and numbered.

I say: "Honestly, it doesn't matter to me. Whatever you want."

"Too bad the Colossus closed. I could go for kebabs."

"Hey, speaking of the Colossus. Kate's mom is opening a restaurant there."

Dad perks up more than I expected at the mention of a new restaurant in town. I mean, places come and go all the time and he never seems to notice. At least once a year someone opens a new restaurant and it's packed for a few months. But eventually the locals drift back to their favorite establishments and the new place ends up closing. One of the disadvantages of small-town living.

"Really? What kind of food is she going to serve?"

"I dunno. She's into fresh produce and fancy ingredients. She makes a sick sandwich."

"And you know this, how?"

"She made me one after school the other day. Roast beef with horseradish mayo."

"Maybe we should invite them down for a barbecue sometime."

He's holding the patio door open and I follow him out to the car — his Volkswagen, not the police cruiser.

"I dunno. You're okay on the grill but, like, Kate's mom's a professional chef."

Dad ignores my comment until we pull out of the driveway.

"I have a few tricks up my sleeve."

"Trust me when I say you're not up to the standard of Kate's mom."

"I may not make sushi rolls but I can still impress the likes of Sally Cooper."

The way he says Sally Cooper makes me swallow, hard. I don't want my dad feeling the same way about Sally Cooper as I do about her daughter. It's just plain creepy to think about.

✗ ✗ ✗

Dad pulls into a parking spot in front of the Dublin Gate Irish Pub. I'm so hungry my stomach is cramping. It's been so long since lunch it might as well have been during the Mesozoic era.

We find an empty table by the front window and before the waitress can ask if we'd like something to drink, I tick off my order: deep-fried mozzarella sticks for a starter, a Pepsi, one pound of extra crispy hot chicken wings, and curly fries. She looks annoyed but turns to Dad. He orders fish and chips, and a beer. Then we sit and look around the restaurant for a few minutes before either of us speaks.

"So how much do you remember about the case? Cooper and McLeod?" I ask.

"I've got a pretty good handle on it."

"You've read a lot of the case notes?"

Dad nods and takes a sip of his Guinness as soon as the waitress slides our drinks across the table, but when he doesn't elaborate, I continue. "I know they searched the Cooper property after the boys went missing. But I'm curious to know why they didn't search any other properties. Like the Goheen property."

"Hindsight, huh? You sound like one of those prank emailers. A few years back I had someone asking the very same question."

"Really?"

"Really. But there was no reason to suspect Peter Goheen. His alibi checked out: he was in all night with his son. There was no evidence back then. Now there's evidence, so we're taking a closer look."

Dad puts his glass down slowly and directs his gaze out the front window. It's an odd move for him because normally he scrutinizes everything I do, like he's carrying out an investigation.

"I understand you're interested in the case, that you've become involved in it, by accident. But now you need to let me do my job."

His eyes snap back to my face and this time I look down at the table. I pick up my glass of Pepsi and take a long drink.

"Every few years someone comes poking around, asking questions about what the police did, what evidence they found, who was a suspect. They'll have read about the case on some online forum and have a theory about what happened. You wouldn't believe the questions we get from total strangers. And suggestions about where to look. As if the police don't know what the hell they're doing."

My mozzarella sticks arrive and I pop one in my mouth before the plate even hits the table. The waitress looks like she's about to say something but then turns away. I immediately regret my gluttony. The thing is so hot I burn my tongue and have to spit it out again. I gulp back half the Pepsi. When I offer one to Dad, he shakes his head.

"I'm having too much fun watching you sear your mouth."

"I'm not questioning your investigative techniques. I just wondered if, like, back then, the police missed something important," I continue while I let the food cool down.

"Well, I think we were pretty thorough. We searched the quarry — the old gravel pit behind the Cooper farm — we dragged the ponds. We searched the uncle and aunt's property, which is where the Corbetts live now, because that was one of the last places they were seen. I think they even checked out the auto body shop by the fire hall. The Coopers used to own it back then."

I finish my mozzarella stick and nod.

We both stop talking when our dinners arrive and I'm grateful for the distraction. The waitress takes my empty plate and offers me another Pepsi.

"Just two glasses of water, please," Dad says.

He sounds a little gruff and the waitress catches my eye. I try to look apologetic but I don't know if she picks up on it. The last thing she needs is a cranky customer. She's just trying to do her job so she can pay the rent or put her kid in hockey, or whatever.

I think maybe Dad will change the topic but he doesn't.

"I want you to promise me you're going to stay out of it. You *and* Kate. The last thing I need is you two hampering the investigation. Please, just trust us to do our jobs."

I stop listening too closely after that, just enough to know when he's finished ranting about not putting anything about the case on social media.

× × ×

When we get home from dinner, I say good night to Dad and head to bed. It's only ten o'clock, but after a long week, my feet feel heavy climbing the stairs and I don't even bother to brush my teeth. All I really want is a dark room and a soft pillow. As soon as I climb under the covers, everything in me settles. Sleep lures me to let go completely, my heartbeat and breathing slow and calm radiates out. I can't wait to lose myself to the comfort of nothingness. I flip over to my other side and turn the pillow in one move, then settle into the cool comfort again. Then I think about Kate — perfect, funny, beautiful. I roll over again and this time I'm awake. My body is revved up and my mind is churning out thoughts faster than those machines that launch baseballs in a batting cage.

I have to bring some game! Something she can't resist. Suddenly an image of the dining room pops into my head. The dusty table surrounded by boxes of case files. I know I shouldn't say anything and that my father would lecture me if he found out, but I can't help myself. I pick up my phone and text.

UR never going to guess what my dad brought home tonight
Kate replies immediately: *What?*
Guess

You said I'd never be able to so just tell me
The case files. Like 30 boxes
On James and Luke????
Yep. He has to review everything. See what they missed to help them nail Peter Goheen
Seriously? So the investigation is back ON!
Looks like it

Kate doesn't reply and my insides turn hollow. I suddenly regret the finality of my last text. *Should I have come up with something wittier? Something to prompt another response?* I watch my phone but no new messages pop up. I flip over to Instagram and scroll through. Josh has posted a selfie from the bus but nothing else is going on. I flip back to my messenger app. Still nothing. I check the time.

I take a long, deep inhale, hold my breath for a count of seven, and exhale as slowly as I can. Then I repeat, until I feel my heartbeat settle again.

My phone buzzes and I pick it up.

Are those files under lock and key? XOX

KATE 7

Saturday morning is a bit of a letdown after my event-filled week. Maybe I'm expecting a hero's breakfast when I wake up, or to find #KateAndZachGetTheJobDone taking over Instagram, but nothing has shifted since we found the skeletons and had a decades-old cold case reopened. There's been no seismic event. Nothing is perceptibly different. The brown water stain on the ceiling still mocks me, the room still smells like old wallpaper and floor polish, and David Bowie is still staring at me with a broody expression.

"Get a new haircut, dude," I say out loud. "That one is *so* 1980s."

I roll over and look out the dusty window. No reporters, no helicopters circling overhead, no people of any size or shape. I'm still stranded in Hicksville, the forgotten metropolis of fourteen thousand people.

I check my phone to see if Zach texted back about the case files but see only my last message and the impulsive XOX I ended with in a rush of excitement. I sigh and bang my phone against my forehead. What was I thinking? Now things are going to be super weird between us.

I flip over to my Instagram account and see that Austin has posted a picture of him at the food court, squeezed between

Serena and some girl I've never seen. There's a cheesy smile on his face. I unfollow his account and block him. "Good riddance," I say to myself, then flip back to see if Zach has texted yet. But nothing.

I envy that Zach is still asleep. I wish I could say the same and make a half-hearted attempt to drop back into dreamland. But it's no use. I'm awake and there's nothing I can do except drag myself out of bed.

I hear Mom in the kitchen when I open my bedroom door. The floor squeaks and she pauses. I tiptoe to the bathroom and shut the door quietly behind me. Maybe I need a few minutes to myself after all, to process the events of the week. Considering the circumstances, you'd think my mind would be full of something more profound, but the most burning question on my mind, annoyingly, is why Zach didn't text back last night. I expected at least some sort of flippant remark about liking him only for the boxes of files, but nothing. Did he even see what I wrote?

I squeeze toothpaste onto my toothbrush and stare down at the sink. There's no getting used to a lavender-colored sink, like ever.

"Kate? Are you up?" Mom calls up the stairs.

I spit, open the door, and yell back, "Just brushing my teeth."

"I'm making waffles with strawberries and whipped cream when you're ready."

I smile to myself. I'm getting a hero's breakfast after all.

When I'm finished with my teeth, I grab the hand mirror and check out the back of my head, which is healing nicely. Then I arrange my hair over the scab until it's barely noticeable and head downstairs.

Mom puts a heaping plate of waffle in front of me when I sit down. She serves herself and sits across from me.

The waffles smell of crispy vanilla and the heat melts the nutmeg-laced cream into rows of delicious little squares. I cut off one corner and stab a strawberry with the tines of my fork. The flavors explode in my mouth like culinary fireworks.

"Did you sleep okay?"

I chew, swallow, nod. "Pretty good. You?"

I shouldn't have asked about her night. It's pretty clear from the dark circles under her eyes that she probably hasn't slept well for a few nights and now she's either going to have to lie or ruin the moment.

"Not so great. Too much on my mind."

"I'm sorry," I say and load up my fork again.

"It's not your fault. I just wish your grandmother was still alive. Or Aunt Kathy was around. Just someone to, you know, sit and talk things through with."

My second bite of waffle tastes a bit more of reality, a bit less of hero. I chew slowly without responding. Mom sips her coffee and cuts a corner off her waffle without eating.

"I was thinking of calling Dad. Maybe you could talk to him?" I say finally.

"If I could have talked to your father about James, I suspect our lives would be very different."

"You and Dad never talked about what happened?"

"Not really."

"Why not?" I pause to imagine what I'd do if something tragic happened to Mom, and who I'd talk to. Zach's goofy face appears in my mind and I've known him less than a week. How could Mom not have talked to her own actual boyfriend?

"The commotion in the weeks after James disappeared was, well, you can't imagine. It turned our lives completely upside down. We broke up shortly after. It was messy. We'd been going out for two years and when you're that age, it feels like it will last forever."

"Did you have a fight?"

"I honestly can't even remember anymore. Or I've just blocked the months afterward. I mean, I remember what happened, in an academic way. Like I rehearsed the events in my mind so I can tell someone what happened first or second. But I can't access the memories the same way. I can't actually remember the days and weeks that followed."

Mom pauses and looks up at me. Her fork is still moving a piece of waffle and strawberry around the plate in a slow circle.

"Does that sound crazy?"

I swallow and offer up a smile. "Not at all. I think stress is like a big eraser. It takes away memories and all sorts of things."

"Smarty pants," she says and drops her fork in exchange for another sip of coffee. "I was so broken about James. It consumed me. Maybe Mitch felt alienated. Or maybe I flipped out at him one day. Who knows?"

"I can ask him," I dare to suggest, and wince, waiting for her demeanor to change. But it doesn't. It's like the fight has drained out of my normally feisty mother.

"Maybe you should. All I remember is that he left town that fall. Then I left a few months later. I just couldn't be here any longer. I had all my credits to graduate so I left to get on with my life. And I didn't come back for a long time. Probably too long. I still feel guilty about that. About leaving Mom. About leaving James's memory behind. When I finally came back it was too late. It was strained. We never really recovered. We'd been close before I left, Mom and I. But when I finally came back, when you were little and I thought you needed to know your family, well, by then it was too late. There was too much distance."

"What about later? Did you and Dad talk about James then, like when you guys got back together and decided to make me?"

I say the last part flippantly. I've always known I was an accident and it's never really bothered me. Mom barely lets a week go by without reminding me I was the best thing that ever happened to her, intentional or not.

"I think we tried to talk but it was a disaster. Your dad has — had — a lot of issues. I'm not just saying that to, I dunno, make myself feel better. I did my best to make it work. I really did. He just had too many demons. His father was so much worse than mine. My dad was cruel when he was drunk. Peter Goheen was just plain evil, drunk and sober. To the core. That must have some sort of a lasting effect on a kid, having a parent like that."

I smear the last bite of waffle around the plate to soak up the remaining whipped cream and strawberry juice.

"Those were good. Thanks."

Mom smiles at me and tilts her head. She doesn't have to say what she's thinking because I already know. But she says it anyway.

"You're a good kid, Kate Cooper. I love you."

"I love you too, Mom. And I'm sorry you have to relive all this stuff. I didn't mean to put you through it again."

She takes her first bite of waffle, chews, and swallows. Then pushes her plate across the table toward me.

"It's okay. I think they call it closure. And if it means Peter Goheen finally sees justice, it'll be worth it." She nods at the plate. "Turns out I'm not really hungry, so help yourself if you want seconds."

She wraps her hands around her mug of coffee and hangs on tight.

After breakfast I go to my room and check my phone. Still nothing from Zach. Annoyed, I text: *WTF? Are you STILL sleeping? It's almost 1. I thought maybe we could hang out today if you ever wake up.*

I lean over and open the window. The smell of fresh-cut grass wafts over my face. It's a smell I've always loved, even though we've never had our own yard before. I wander over to the bulletin board and start to unpin the concert tickets and stack them in a pile. I unpin dried corsages and a strip of small black-and-white photos of Mom and some long-forgotten friend. I put everything into a restaurant-supply-store box and take it into James's room. Then I go back and pack up the rest of the room until the only things left are mine — and David Bowie. For some reason I can't get rid of David.

I'm in the middle of dusting when my phone vibrates. I lunge to pick it up.

Sorry. Awake now. What's up?

Do you always sleep til 2?

Dad usually wakes me up by now but he's distracted. What's up?

Cleaning my room. I found a creepy doll under the bed

Chucky?

Similar but with a beanbag body

Anything else?

Lots of dust bunnies. Old school notebooks. Turns out Mom was a pretty good creative writer. Twisted plotlines but good dialogue and character arc

You cleaning all day?

No

You still wanna do something?

Like what?

I dunno. Netflix at your place?

Mom will hover

Video games at my place?

I'll come down in about an hour. Also do you guys have an old cassette player?

Yep. An old Walkman. Still works. You know Dad doesn't own anything made after 1990. Besides me

Can I borrow it?

Sure thing

✕ ✕ ✕

Before I head over to Zach's, I check the time difference between me and Australia. It's super early for Dad but there's never a good time to call Australia so I hit dial and hope for the best.

"Kate!" he answers brightly, as if the Gold Coast sunshine has penetrated his skull and altered his early morning personality. "Twice in one month. Is everything okay?"

"Twice in one year!" I counter. "Soon I won't be able to refer to you as my *estranged* father."

"Very funny. But seriously. Is everything okay?"

"Sure. I just called to update you."

The line is silent and the speech I have planned escapes me. In the background I can hear a voice, a woman's voice.

"Is someone there?" I ask.

"My girlfriend," Dad replies. "Theresa."

I roll my eyes and don't ask.

Dad prompts, "You said you wanted to update me on something? You didn't go back to my father's place, I hope."

"Well, it turns out I did."

"Kate!"

"Hold on. Before you get upset. That's why I'm calling. I thought you'd want to know that they found some remains on your dad's property. In a cave. Two sets actually. They took a DNA sample from Mom."

"For real?"

"For real, Dad. My friend, Zach, and I found them actually. And we told his dad, who's a detective. And the police got a search warrant and went and searched the cave. They got the bodies. Well, skeletons really. It's not looking good for your dad, I'm afraid. He's in custody." I pause and listen. Then: "Are you okay?"

Dad clears his throat. His voice wavers and catches. He pauses then continues.

"I'm fine. Shocked, I guess."

"They think it's Mom's brother, James. And his friend, Luke."

"That makes sense," Dad says so softly I can hardly hear him.

"So you didn't know the boys were there all this time?"

"Of course I didn't know," he says, a little too harshly. Then he softens again. "How's your mom?"

I lean across the bed to look out the window, down the long driveway that ends at a rural road, and beyond that at farm fields stretching into the distance. There's so much space around me, I shiver. It just doesn't feel right.

"She's coping," I say. "I mean, it's a lot to process. We just moved back here so there's all that to deal with. And also her parents' stuff everywhere. Then this. I think she wishes she had someone to talk to. Like someone else who remembers her brother. Like to reminisce with, or whatever."

"I can only imagine," he says quietly. "Although I'm not sure I'm the right person."

"I didn't mean to suggest ... Or maybe I did. I dunno. But if you think about it, really, there's no righter person. Maybe you can come back for a bit?"

I've never asked my father for much, or asked much of my father. So part of me hopes I can cash in my chips, so to speak.

"I'll think about it. And text you later. But I need to go right now. Sorry. I don't mean to rush you off the phone or anything. I'm glad you called," my father says.

"No worries. Take care. I guess say hi to Theresa for me."

"I will. Tell your mother I'm sorry."

"Normally messages from you don't elicit feelings of warmth so I may play that one by ear. But I appreciate the sentiment."

He chuckles, a low, deep noise almost like a purr. Now that the call is wrapping up and I know he's not alone, for some reason, I suddenly feel like an outsider. Although we joke and kid each other, we aren't close. And although I'd never admit it to anyone, not even Zach, I wish I knew him better. I wish he knew me better.

ZACH 8

Monday morning, Kate falls into the seat beside me on the bus without hesitation. It's as if we've been seatmates since grade school. I glance back at Josh and our eyes meet briefly before he turns to talk to the other guys. The good news is that even from that glancing look, I know Josh is never going to be pissed at me. I mean, I kind of already knew since he pretty much gave me permission where Kate is concerned, but I feel a little guilt nibbling at my conscience just the same. It can't feel good when your best friend stops sitting with you on the bus, no matter the reason.

"Did your dad say anything about the case this weekend?" Kate asks when the bus groans forward.

"Still waiting for DNA results. How's your mom?" I say under my breath so nobody can overhear.

"She's trying to let on that she's okay but she's really not. Anyhow, I have to show you something!"

Kate pulls my father's ancient yellow Walkman out of her backpack, the one I lent her the other day. It's about the size of a brick and made of hard plastic. She puts the headphones over my ears and presses play. I hear some shuffling sounds and someone clear their throat. Then a voice comes through, a young voice, male. It starts off with a squeak then deepens.

"Welcome to *Rock 'n Roll Hour with DJ James*. Sit back and enjoy the ride. First up, last year's number five top song, 'Don't Stop Believin'' by Journey."

I hit stop and pull the headphones off my ears. Kate is looking at me with shining eyes, a smile playing with the corners of her mouth.

"Is that really him?" I ask.

Kate nods enthusiastically. "It is. He made this mixed tape his last summer, apparently. And he introduces every song like he's some hotshot DJ. It's so cool. And it makes me feel, I dunno, more connected to him."

"Has your mom listened?"

"Not yet. I want to get it transferred to something more permanent. Who knows how long this old cassette will last? Apparently the ribbons get brittle. So I'm going to loop all the speaking parts together into one sequence."

Kate takes the Walkman and wraps the earphone cord around the yellow plastic casing before handing it to me.

"Thanks for the loaner. I wanted you to hear his voice. So he'd feel real to you too. He was funny, you know? At the end of the cassette, on the second side, he finishes with this deep, cheesy DJ persona: *This is DJ James closing it down, folks. But don't worry. You can flip this thing over and start again!*"

Kate laughs at this memory and shakes her head. She's just in the middle of telling me about a gadget she ordered from Amazon that converts cassettes to MP3s when I notice someone hanging over the back of our seat. It's Josh and he hands me his phone, open at Facebook.

"Since you never check your account, I thought you should see this."

He shows me the feed for the town's Facebook page. Normally it's the place where people post missing pet notices, couches for sale, school concerts, and community events. But the post Josh shows me is a series of aerial photos, probably taken from someone's drone, of the Goheen property. It's posted from an account called *Justice for James and Luke*. I flick through the photos and it suddenly hits me how seriously Dad has been underplaying the investigation. The property is swarming with people and police cars. The post reads: *A break in a thirty-five-year-old cold case? Remains of two individuals recovered. Elderly man in custody.*

When I flip over to see who has posted this, the first thing I notice is that it's a brand-new Facebook account. There are no previous posts, but the account already has over two hundred followers.

I show the page to Kate and she immediately takes out her phone.

"Is it in the news yet?"

"Maybe not officially, but it won't take long," Josh says.

"Wow," I say and start reading through a string of comments, some by people I know and some by complete strangers.

My prayers go out to the families.
You will always be in our hearts, Luke.
Finally, some answers.
Is this the Goheen property?
    Yep. Peter Goheen. He's a total scumbag.
    I always had my suspicions about him.
    Hope he rots in prison.

Innocent til proven guilty, folks.
Heard two kids busted open the case. Is it true?
Yeah. Couple of high school kids apparently. WTF?

After reading the last comment, Kate and I exchange awkward looks.

Josh's jaw unhinges. "Shit, are *you* guys the two kids?"

I motion for him to keep his voice down, and he leans closer.

"It was a total fluke," I say. "But keep it to yourself. If it gets out it could, like, compromise the investigation or something. And Dad would murder *me*."

Kate scowls at me, but I don't try to explain. I don't really know if anything could compromise the investigation, but I do know that if Dad finds out I've been talking about one of his cases at school, I'm in deep shit.

Josh grabs his phone back as the bus pulls up to the school and files off ahead of Kate and me. Teenagers are generally phone obsessed, but today the scene is shocking. Every single student is looking at their phone as they mingle outside in small groups. Even those walking into the building are deep into Facebook, Instagram, Twitter. It's a repeat inside the school. Kids are standing silently at their lockers, heads hanging forward, phones pressed close to their faces. I've never seen the hallways so still. Every now and then someone looks up, then turns back to their phone. By the time I open Facebook on my own phone, *Justice for James and Luke* has 322 followers and the comments are appearing so fast it's hard to keep up with what's being posted.

"How long will it take before someone figures out it's us for reals?" Kate whispers. She looks uneasy.

"Hopefully never," I say.

"It's bad enough being the new kid, and the kid with the dead uncle. But to be one of the kids who found the bodies? I don't think I can handle that much notoriety."

My stomach lurches. As much as Kate dreads others finding out, I also don't want that news getting to Mom. She'd be all over Dad, and Dad would be all over me. And, well, the outcome would straight up suck.

I scroll through the comments and type: *As if a couple of high schoolers are going to break a cold case.*

Kate follows with: *Fake news if I ever heard any.*

Josh does a solid and jumps in with: *Wasn't any stupid kids. It was the police for sure. I saw police cars out there last week.*

Josh is closing his locker when I look up. I'm about to mouth the word *thanks*, but he nods before I have a chance. That guy always has my back.

When I get to com tech class, two girls are talking about the dead guys the police found in some old dude's house. I listen with amusement as the story morphs moment by moment. By the time the teacher walks in, the two dead guys were sitting on the living room couch and Mr. Goheen was playing a game of poker with them. The absurdity of the rumors actually makes me feel better. It'll be impossible for anyone to know the truth with so much bullshit floating around.

Kate texts: *Apparently my grandfather was a cannibal and had the bodies in his freezer?*

I heard they were your twin uncles. Born with severe deformities and kept hidden from the world until they died under suspicious circumstances.

Kind of funny hearing all these stories we know aren't true.

Yep. Don't think "two high school kids found the remains" can compete with cannibalism and twin hunchback uncles :P

I just hope nobody figures out it's my grandfather's property.

Nah, how can they?

Definitely no telling anyone about When You Dare to Date Kate.

Why not?

People will put 2 and 2 together and get 100. Last thing I need right now.

Gotcha, I text, along with the zippered-lip emoji.

✗ ✗ ✗

I'm walking back to my locker after com tech when Josh pulls me aside.

"Thanks for that Facebook comment," I say.

"No problem. Anytime. But I just saw something weird."

"What?" I ask, wondering what can be weirder than finding two skeletons in a crevasse.

"I was checking out Kate's Instagram profile and, you know, seeing who her friends are. And one of them is a *Mitch* Goheen."

My heart sinks. This is why I hate social media. I pull Josh close and whisper: "That's her dad. She doesn't see him much."

"That means the dog killer is her *grandfather*?"

"Shhhh. Yeah. But keep it to yourself. She'd never even met him before moving here." I'm starting to feel defensive.

"That's so weird. I mean, she just arrived in town like, what, two weeks ago? And then this? She finds a couple of dead bodies?"

"Like I said, it was just an accident."

"Still, people are going to figure it out pretty soon. You should tell her to block her father. I mean, she can unblock him later when everything blows over. But if you don't want people figuring out the connection that's what I'd recommend."

Like I said, Josh is a great guy and always has my back. And Kate's too, apparently.

✘ ✘ ✘

During English, when I'm supposed to be writing in my journal, I sneak a look at the Facebook account *Justice for James and Luke*. The number of followers has jumped to 412 and there's a comment about the drone photos from someone named CJ Grover that stands out, at least to me.

Hope they look in the drive shed this time.

I don't know why it screams at me but it does and I immediately text Kate to check out the comments from the last half hour. Then I watch for her reaction. She scrolls through slowly, reading, pauses, then looks at me with narrowed eyebrows. It's like we've hit the jackpot.

Bleachers at lunch? I text.

She sends back a thumbs-up emoji.

✘ ✘ ✘

"Did you see it?" I call down to Kate as she climbs the bleachers toward me. She's carrying her lunch — no doubt some fancy creation her mother made that's going to put my salami sandwich to shame.

She doesn't respond but sits down and pulls her hair into a ponytail.

"You saw that comment from CJ Grover, right?" I ask again.

Kate nods.

"Whaddya think that's all about?"

"I dunno. Why mention the drive shed specifically?" Kate asks. "Unless you *know* it's important."

"Maybe if you want to draw people away from the real evidence?" I suggest.

"Either way it has to be someone close to the case. Like, who do you think took the photos of the Goheen property? And with a drone?"

"That's a mystery for sure. You don't have a drone, do you?" I ask.

Kate smirks. "My style is up close and personal."

We turn back to the Facebook page and the *Justice for James and Luke* follower count has jumped to 508.

"That must just about be the whole of Hicksville."

"Hicksville?"

"Sorry. My father's pet name for Clarendon."

"Clarendon's not that bad. You just have to give it a chance."

✗ ✗ ✗

That night, as I'm lying in bed cataloguing images of Kate's face in my brain, my phone vibrates. I pick it up to see she's sent a text. I know it's goofy, but just seeing her name pop up makes me smile so wide I think my face might split in two.

U there?

Yep

Sitting down?

I type *In bed*, delete, then type *Lying down.*

Are you in bed? she asks.

Yep

Remember the post about the drive shed?

Yep

I just remembered something.

What?

James's initials were JC.

And?

The post was written by CJ Grover.

That's a stretch, I point out.

Yeah, but his imaginary friend when he was little was Grover.

I sit up in bed suddenly and drop my phone. "Seriously?" I say out loud. Then I fumble the phone back into my hands and type.

Did you check out his profile page?

Doing that now.

?????

Privacy settings tight. Gonna have to send a friend request.

Urgggg

✕ ✕ ✕

By Friday, Kate still hasn't heard back from CJ Grover on Facebook. The DNA and other forensic tests are still being processed and I can't get any information out of my father no matter how many lines of questioning I try. After all the excitement it feels as if the case has stalled and Kate is as annoyed and frustrated as I am. We try to drown our sorrows in video games, but even a three-hour marathon doesn't help us forget we're just putting in time.

"Patience has never really been my strongest character trait." Kate scowls. She tosses the controller on the coffee table and sinks deep into the couch. "I can't stand all the waiting. I'm going crazy. I can't concentrate on school. I can't eat. We have to do something."

"Like what?"

"I dunno. But if it wasn't for us, nothing would have happened in the first place. So maybe we need to speed things up again."

"I get the sense you have a plan?"

Kate flashes her megawatt smile and my heart thumps hard against my rib cage, like Swifer wagging his tail when he sees Josh get off the school bus.

"We need to go back to the property and find that drive shed or whatever. I'm sure there's something there we need to find."

"You're out of your mind. We can't go back there and start looking around."

"Why not? My grandfather's in custody. So we don't have to be afraid of running into him. And maybe I can get some useful footage …"

I don't hesitate to point out that the property is swarming with police and Kate looks at me like I'm the biggest bummer around. It's a look I've seen her flash her mother, which is probably the point.

"They aren't going to hurt us! I mean, maybe they'll kick us off the property and scold us if they find us. But by then we might have found something important," she presses.

"You remember that my dad's a detective, right? Like there's no way I won't get in a shit load of trouble if we get caught?"

"So let's not get caught. You can't always expect the worst to happen, Zach. You need to chill."

Kate pulls out her phone and pulls up a satellite map of the area.

"Look," she says, leaning so close I can smell the vanilla scent of her hair. It reminds me of an ice-cream sundae and a warm hug all at once. "I wasn't suggesting we walk up the driveway in the middle of the day. But if we came from this side, through this clearing here, then through these trees, we'd come right out at these buildings. The big one's obviously a barn. But this other one over on the left, it's probably that drive shed we need to get into." She traces the route on the satellite image.

I can't help but protest. The stakes are so much higher for me. "We don't know for sure we need to get into the drive shed at all. It could be a total psych."

"You're right. It could be. But there's only one way to know for sure." Kate pockets her phone and presses the palms of her hands together as if in prayer. When I don't respond right away, she pouts a little.

I sigh and my shoulders slump slightly. "Did you have a plan for when we might do this?"

"Are you busy tonight?"

KATE 8

Ideas always seem better in the light of day. Somehow, darkness casts a sinister shadow over reason and logic. At least that's what happens to me when Zach texts to say he's at the end of our driveway with the bikes. My heart drops hard and feels like a hunk of cement in my chest; I have to fight just to breathe. It weighs heavy on all my organs, crushing my stomach until I feel like throwing up. It was always like this out west when I was staring down an abandoned building at night, but the promise of a viral video propelled me. Now I will my body to move — down the stairs, out the door, and into the night. *You've done this before, Kate Cooper*, I tell myself. *You can do it again.*

The ride to the Goheen property feels longer than before. My legs feel like lead, or like I'm pedaling uphill and through water at the same time. I know it's the dread weighing me down. But still, I keep moving. Something pushes me so I can't even consider giving up and turning around.

Instead of approaching from the front of the property like we did before, we ride past the first road and around to the next concession so we can slip through the back of the property. From this direction, we'll come across the barn and outbuildings without getting anywhere near the police barricades, which, according to the aerial photos on Facebook and Instagram, surround the rock outcropping and cave.

Zach takes the lead across a field without hesitating. Apparently growing up in Clarendon means you have no irrational fear of dark, wild places at night. I follow his footsteps and shadowy form moving an arm's length ahead. The moon is a bloated crescent, a half circle glowing like the outline of Santa's belly above and casting the palest light down on our movements. I look up and think, as I always do, that my significance in the universe is merely a pixel on the Imax-sized movie screen of life.

Zach stops to check his map app and I step close. I put my hand on the small of his back for comfort and feel body heat radiating through his shirt. With just the slight touch of my fingers, I can tell his back is strong and sinewy. I can feel the ripples of muscle over bone, and when I recall the broadness of his shoulders, I feel a wash of affection flood through me, catching me off guard. I shiver in the cool night air.

"You okay?" he turns and asks quietly, almost a whisper, which feels more intimate than I'm sure he intends.

I nod and then, realizing he can't see me clearly in the dark, say, "Yeah, of course." My words evaporate into the night, leaving me to hope he didn't detect the tremble in my voice.

I pull my sweater closed and zipper it against the dampness hanging in the tall grasses. Then I pull up my hood too.

"It's chilly tonight," I whisper.

"I guess fall is finally on its way." He extends the glowing phone toward me and I peer down at it. "About another five hundred yards until we hit the tree line. Good thing you wore pants. I expect there're going to be some major brambles to get through."

By the time we reach the trees, my pants are wet from the thighs down, and no doubt the dewy grass would show the path we took across the field if there was a full moon: a dark line through the silvery gray. We pick our way through the trees, staying close enough that I can smell Zach's deodorant even when I can't see him clearly. He seems to have a natural sense of direction but I feel completely turned around. If I was left on my own, I have no doubt I would walk in circles until daybreak.

When we come to the clearing, I see the barn and farmhouse in the distance. The house is dark, not even the porch light is on, and all of the windows are black. It hovers like a shadow against the coal-gray sky and I shiver, wondering about the years my father lived there, trapped. I wonder what went on behind those walls to make him so remote, so inaccessible. I know it's not that women don't like him. He's always had girlfriends — like Theresa. So many, in fact, I've lost track. I wonder if this one will stick for the long run.

I think about the pictures of my father hanging on the wall and wish I had a way to get in and see them up close. But I know breaking into an old man's house is not on the night's agenda. After another minute of sneaking through the darkness, I stop and video my surroundings. I squint with the hopes of improving my night vision. Tucked behind the barn is a little building that I assume is the drive shed.

"C'mon," I say, tugging Zach's arm. "I think that's the one we're looking for."

Zach turns off his phone and we move quietly under the

shadowy cover of night. The building looks like a garage, but the walls are made of weathered barn board and the doors open out instead of up. The weeds have grown up high around it and the path to the doors is almost undetectable. Zach wades through to a single side door and pulls on the metal handle with both hands. He has to lean backward before he can budge it at all. Eventually it groans open and he slips inside. Before following, I run my hand over the outside wall: the wood is worn smooth from decades of sun and rain and snow.

"Are you coming?" Zach hisses from inside.

I take one last scan of my surroundings, listen for any sounds of human activity, and, satisfied that we're alone on this part of the property, slide inside behind Zach and close the door. There are no windows, so in comparison to the outside, the darkness in the drive shed is total. It seeps around every curve of my body and encompasses me.

"Don't move," Zach says. "Who knows what's in here."

He fumbles with his phone and turns on the flashlight, then sweeps the light from one side of the space to the other. Other than a stack of old buckets and a few broken farm implements, the drive shed is empty. It smells like years of neglect: rotting wood mingled with dust and dampness.

"What are we even looking for?" he asks. His voice sounds abrupt in the close darkness.

"Beats me," I whisper. "But there must be something we need to find."

I activate my phone's flashlight and begin to scan one side of the space while Zach scans the other. Inch by inch.

Other than cobwebs there's not much. I find a musty copy of the *Farmers' Almanac* from 1978, its pages thick with moisture, and a Planters Peanut tin of nuts and bolts, thick ones like the kind used on heavy machinery.

At the back of the shed is a door with a rusty padlock hanging loose on the hasp. I pull off the padlock, then open the door to peer inside at a small room with a wooden workbench against the far wall. The air is cooler in the small room, dusty, still. It feels like what I imagine a tomb would be like inside. The thought runs up my spine and scurries around my neck. It takes all of my courage to step inside. I flash the light up at the low, angled ceiling. It's wooden like the walls, but nails are visible through the boards, like whoever shingled the building couldn't be bothered to get the right length of nails.

The workbench is scattered with rusted tools, covered in an inch of dust and mouse poop. I shoot a few seconds of video, then aim the phone up and down. Unlike the exposed dirt in the drive shed, the workshop floor is made of wide wooden planks. From the looks of it, the door has been smashed open at some point because the wood is splintered around the bottom hinge. I wonder if this is the clue we're supposed to find. Is there something hidden beneath the wooden floor?

I walk carefully over each of the wooden planks to see if any of them are loose, but none of them shifts under my weight. Next, I look through the tools on the workbench, raising a cloud of dust in the process. When I start to sneeze, Zach appears.

"You okay?"

"It's super dusty," I explain, and sneeze again, as if for emphasis.

"Anything in here?"

"Just a pile of old tools that look like they haven't been used in a hundred years."

Zach flashes his light over the workbench. Above it, a small grimy window lets in the dimmest wash of moonlight. There's nothing that looks like evidence.

"The door looks like it's been kicked in at some point," I offer.

Zach closes and examines the door, but then moves away without comment. I can tell he doesn't think it's what we're meant to find either.

As in the larger room, we scan the walls with our flashlights, looking for something that might be important, something that means something or tells us something we don't already know. I climb under the workbench to scan the walls and floor there. And that's when I see markings carved into the thick square leg of the workbench, on the back side facing the wall. It would be easy to miss. But the light from my phone picks up the deep curve of an "R" beneath a coating of dust.

RIP
LM
JC
8 26 82

"Zach! Oh my God. I found something."

My heart is pounding so hard in my chest, I can feel the vibrations going up my throat. I start to tremble when he climbs under the workbench beside me.

"Look! This inscription. The initials and the date."

I take a photo with my phone but don't dare run my fingers over the letters, even though I so badly want to touch them to be sure they're real and not my mind playing tricks.

Zach reads the message aloud. "RIP. That's pretty obvious. And then the initials for Luke McLeod and James Cooper. It must be the day they ..." he says, then asks, "What day did they disappear?"

"I forget. Sometime at the end of summer. I'm pretty sure it was 1982. So the date fits."

"I think it was the twenty-sixth, I think that's what the newspaper article says. And if it is, then we know ..." Zach pauses in the middle of his hypothesis.

"We know what?"

"I'm not sure."

"But who would have carved this? And when?" I pause. "And why?"

I climb out from under the bench and send the photo to Zach. His phone vibrates but he doesn't respond. He's quietly unraveling the meaning of what we just found.

I stare at the photo on my phone. No matter how I twist my imagination, nothing becomes clear, nothing fits a reasonable pattern. Could it have been my mother? My father? My grandfather? None of these options seems to make sense. If it was a goodbye message, then why would someone inscribe it into the leg of a workbench in a falling-down drive shed?

"I can't think clearly in here. Let's go home and figure this out," Zach says finally. "Unless you want to shoot more footage?" He stands up and wipes the dirt off the knees of his jeans.

"Nah. This isn't going to work. Too small. The house on the other hand ..."

Zach doesn't let me finish. "No way. Definitely not."

And I give in before I even get started. I know there's no way we can break into my grandfather's house, even if my curiosity is screaming at me to get inside.

"C'mon," Zach says and nudges me gently.

We reach for the door handle at the same time, then stop with our hands in midair. The sound of the drive shed door creaking open sets my heart pounding again. Instinctively we both turn off our phones and our hands find each other in the dark. I squeeze tight and Zach steps in front of me.

Stray beams of light sneak through holes and cracks in the wall. Someone is in the drive shed with a high-powered flashlight, and although I can't hear footsteps, I can tell the light is moving toward the workshop.

Please don't be Zach's dad, I think to myself. *Any other cop but Detective Whitchurch.*

I press myself against the wall behind the door, hoping whoever is two feet away will somehow leave without discovering us. *It's possible*, I tell myself. *It's possible they'll glance in and leave without looking behind the door.*

The door swings open and I try to melt into the wall. Zach squeezes tight against me. Then the person steps into the workshop. Whoever is there, I can hear their breathing and smell something familiar — the scent of Polo aftershave put on a bit too strong.

I'm trying to place the scent when the flashlight scans across the wall and then over Zach and I cowering in the corner.

"Jesus!"

The man jumps back when his flashlight beam lands on us. I can't see a thing with the stream of light in my face, but when he shouts, "What the hell?" I let go of Zach's hand and block the brightness from boring into my eyes. It's definitely not a cop on the other end of that flashlight. I step forward and squint.

"What the hell? Dad?"

The light moves down to my feet then back up to my face.

"Kate? What are you doing here?" he asks crossly.

"I was just about to ask you the same thing," I fire back. "I mean, at least I'm in my country of residence."

"At least I'm not trespassing," he points out.

A quick glance at Zach reveals how absolutely freaked out he is. His eyes are wide and his jaw unhinges in the classic cartoon look of disbelief.

"Are you sure about that?" I challenge, swallowing my anxiety. "When exactly was the last time you were here? Or even in the country? A couple decades ago?"

We're in a standoff, both bristling and on edge. If we had guns, they'd be pointed at one another's heads.

"You asked me to come here!"

"And when have you ever done anything I wanted?"

I glance around suspiciously and wonder what exactly he has come home for and why his first stop is the drive shed. But I don't ask. I can't. I can't risk him asking questions of us either. So instead of continuing to accuse each other of being in the wrong place, we stand across the workshop from one another. And we stare at each other. And my heart pounds an irrational beat inside my chest.

ZACH 9

Kate and her father stare at each other for a full five minutes before either of them moves or speaks. It's weird because they barely blink and the only one who seems to feel seriously awkward about the whole situation is me. It's the longest five minutes of my life. Finally, her dad opens his arms tentatively, as if he's not sure if he should be offering a hug or if Kate will respond appropriately. At first, I think she's going to snub him completely. She pauses, assesses, sizes him up. Then, finally, she steps close for a strained embrace. It takes a couple of tries for them to figure out where to put their arms, and some jockeying while they figure out how close to stand and for how long. Kate makes the first move by stepping back slightly, then her father drops his arms as if the whole thing is a regrettable mistake.

"You came for a surprise visit?" Kate says finally.

"Yeah. I thought I should, you know? Come and see how you're doing with everything that's going on."

"When were you going to let me know you were here?"

"In the morning. It's late. I didn't want to wake you."

Kate scowls and shifts her weight from one foot to another. She's not buying a word he's selling, and from the way he looks down at the ground and inscribes small circles around his feet with the flashlight, it's obvious he knows it too.

"It's nice to know you care. I mean, I didn't know James so it's not too hard for me. But Mom could definitely use some support."

"I can only imagine what she's going through. That's another reason I decided to come, well, so quickly." His words hang, suspended like dust motes, in the cool, dank air.

"Are you going to see your father?"

Kate's dad swallows hard. "I don't know. I haven't decided." He glances at me briefly, as if he's finally noticed me standing there.

He puts his hand forward to shake.

"Mitch Goheen," he says and squeezes my hand hard when I offer it to him.

"Zach Whitchurch." My voice squeaks and I clear my throat before saying, "Nice to meet you."

Mitch looks around the workshop nervously and glances back at the door like there's something there he'd rather that we don't see.

"Do you guys want to get out of here? It's not exactly the best place for catching up with your favorite daughter," he says, spreading on a heavy layer of charm.

Kate steps past him and out the door, leaving nothing for us to do but follow.

"Did you rent a car?" she asks, sweeping her phone's flashlight across the yard. I want to remind her that we're technically trespassing and trying to remain undetected, but I'm afraid of her hostility turning on me instead.

"Yeah. It's up by the house."

Kate glances toward the house, which is still sitting in complete darkness.

"You didn't go in? You're not spending the night?"

Mitch snorts. "I got a room at the hotel in town."

"Did you see any cops on your way in?"

He shakes his head. "Not by the house. There was a cruiser further down the road."

We stand clustered in the middle of the dark yard, the slice of moon splashing pale light over us. I glance this way and that, anxious to get moving, to get as far away from the property as possible. Kate picks up on my nervous energy.

"Can you at least give us a lift home?"

"Uh, sure. Where's Zach live?" He glances at me as though I'm a child who can't speak for himself.

"Next door to us."

"The McLeod place?"

"Yeah. Weird, huh?" she says this aggressively, like he'd know more if he was around more and she resents him for living on the other side of the world.

Mitch's discomfort grows visibly. He pulls a cell phone out of his back pocket and glances at the time.

"Listen. We need to get on the same page. It's after eleven and I'm guessing your mother doesn't know you're over here in the middle of the night with your ..." he glances at me again and I look down at my feet in response, "... friend, Zach. If we walk into the house now there're going to be major fireworks."

Kate nods and for the moment it feels like they've struck a truce, like they're on the same team. But only because they have a common adversary.

"Let's get to the car and figure this out. If we see any cops, Zach has to stay out of sight," she says.

Mitch looks at me with the furrowed brow of a skeptic. "Why? Does he have a record or something?"

Kate smiles wryly. "No, but his dad's a detective."

I can tell she takes delight from the look of alarm that flashes across her father's face. But Mitch quickly regains his composure and flicks off his flashlight.

"C'mon," he says and heads toward the house. "The car's this way." There's nothing to do but pocket our phones and follow.

"Before we go home, can we swing by and pick up our bikes?" Kate asks as she trails behind him.

"You rode your bikes over here in the dark?" he asks over his shoulder.

"Dad! Hello! I'm fifteen! How else would I get here?"

He shoots her a sideways glance then unlocks the car with a *beep beep* that makes me wince. So much for being stealthy.

We've just Tetris-ed the bikes into the trunk and climbed inside the car when Kate's phone goes off. Our nerves are so frayed we all jump in our seats and my heart lodges in my throat. There's only one person who could be calling.

Kate pulls the phone out of her pocket and swears.

"Your mom?" Mitch asks knowingly.

She nods but doesn't answer. She stares at it while it rings and vibrates in her hand.

"Quick. Answer," I urge. "Before she hangs up and calls my dad."

Kate takes a deep breath, then answers with a tentative, "Hey, Mom."

On the other end, Sally is anything but tentative. Kate holds the phone away from her ear and Mitch and I can hear every-thing she's saying, or screaming, over the line.

When the strength of Sally's anger levels off, Kate finally gets a chance to speak.

"Are you ready to listen now?" She puts the phone back up to her ear. "You're right. I shouldn't have snuck out without letting you know where I was going. I know I'm only fifteen. No, I'm not at the Goheen property. Yes, I'm with Zach. I'll tell him to call his dad right away."

Kate looks back at me while she bobs her head up and down with the phone at her ear. My heart sinks low. We've both been caught.

"It's not just the two of us. I'm also with Dad. Yes, *my* dad. Mitch? He came home unexpectedly. I know, he should have let us both know."

She glances over at Mitch and he rolls his eyes.

"We're just having a coffee. We'll be home in about thirty minutes. I know it's almost midnight. But I haven't seen him in, like, two years."

Kate pauses, listens, bites her thumbnail.

"Can we talk about that when I get home? Dad's dropping me off. He wants to know if he should come in and say hi."

She switches the phone to her other hand and other ear.

"I'll tell him. We're just finishing up. See you soon."

She drops her phone onto her lap and sinks her head into her hands.

"Zach, you better call your dad. Apparently, he's freaking out." Her words are muffled.

"I'll text him," I suggest.

"Whatever. I can only deal with one lunatic parent at a time," she says, then lifts her face toward Mitch and adds, "No offense."

"None taken. So am I coming in now to say hi, or what?"

"If you don't mind. Yes. But she's not exactly in the best mood, obviously. You might as well deliver Zach to his individual hell first."

Mitch drives slowly down the dark road. There isn't another car in sight and I lean close to the window to look up at the stars blinking above.

"Did you go to Clarendon High School?" I ask Mitch, suddenly, randomly.

Mitch brakes for a pothole and the bikes jostle in the trunk.

"No. I went to school in the city. We didn't live here full time. I mean, my father spent most of his time in that place. But while Mom was alive we went back and forth between there and our house in the city. Then after, well, I went to boarding school and just came for holidays and weekends."

"So that was like your country house?"

"Something like that," Mitch says evasively, leaving me to wonder what he's not saying.

"So you didn't know my dad?"

"I didn't really know many people around here at all. I knew Sally because our fathers were friends. And I met a few kids through her. But mostly I just hung out with her or kept to myself. Sometimes I brought friends with me for the weekend."

Mitch drives slowly and turns onto Valley Road. He glances at the Cooper farm as he creeps past.

"Wow. It really does look the same. I don't think anything's changed."

"Wait until you see inside." Kate fake gags on two fingers.

Dad's car is there when Mitch pulls into our driveway and I hope he doesn't come out of the house. The last thing I want is to get told off by my father in front of Kate's father. But of course, I'm not that lucky. Mitch is lifting the second bike from the trunk when the mudroom door swings open and Dad steps out. He's still in his uniform. It only takes him about six strides before he's at the car. He doesn't address me but turns to Mitch.

"Thanks for bringing my son home."

Mitch straightens up and puts the bike on the ground. Face to face, he and Dad are about the same height, but Mitch is broader, cooler, definitely more handsome. I see a look on my dad's face that I know all too well. It's the recognition that Sally Cooper is way out of Dad's league, and if I wasn't afraid of what I had coming, I'd step close and put my arm around his shoulder in a show of solidarity. Instead, I keep myself busy with wheeling the bikes over to lean against the deck railing.

I wonder if Dad's going to say anything to Mitch about his dad being in custody, or the cold case in general. But he doesn't. Instead he says, "I don't think we've ever met before," and introduces himself as Al Whitchurch, not as Detective Whitchurch. It's a friendly gesture.

Mitch introduces himself and they shake hands.

"I'm sorry to be meeting under these circumstances," Mitch says, and again, I really want to like this guy. He may be a bit on the gray side of grunge rock, but at least he has class. Mitch flips the hair out of his face with his hand and offers a conspiratorial smile. He nods toward the car where Kate sits staring straight ahead. "I really should get this one home too."

Dad steps back and Mitch climbs into the car. Kate and I share a look of dread before Mitch reverses down the driveway and pulls onto the road. I watch the car lights sweep up the hill before Dad says: "It's too late to get into it tonight but this is not over."

"I know," I say, hanging my head in a show of mock shame, and drag myself inside. "See you tomorrow."

Upstairs in my room, before I plug in my phone to charge and climb into bed, I text Kate: *You still alive?*

She responds right away: *Yep*

In bed?

Yep. Mitch and Mom are downstairs talking.

Mitch?

Mitch. Dad. Whatever. He's not really the fatherly type.

Was it bad?

Not great but short at least. How about for you?

Deferred til tomorrow

Lucky you

Did you ever find out what he was doing in the drive shed?

Nope. But then again. He never found out what we were doing either :)

I pause, trying to decide what to text next. Finally, I send: *Maybe see you tomorrow?*

A thumbs-up emoji and *Sweet dreams* are the last things I see before I fall asleep.

KATE 9

Because we've never lived in the same country before, let alone the same city, Dad has never picked me up at the door. Normally we meet at an airport and go back to whichever place he's living. Then we spend our two weeks ordering in Thai food and hanging out at the beach. So it's super awkward when we're all standing on the front porch the next day, trying to figure out the etiquette of the *handoff*.

"Have a nice day together," Mom says for the third time while Dad looks around the porch and scratches the scruff on his neck.

I lean in for a goodbye hug and it takes two tries before Mom and I get our heads in the right position to embrace. When I step back, Dad steps forward, like he's next in line for a hug, but Mom turns away and it's hard to tell if it's a deliberate brush-off. He shoves his hands deep into his front pockets and hunches his shoulders up around his ears.

We cross the lawn and I half turn to see if Mom is still watching us, which she is, so I wave a little and she waves back, then she disappears through the door as if the house has swallowed her whole.

"What do you want to do?" he asks the second our bums hit the car seats.

My brain scrambles.

"I dunno? I've only been here, like, three weeks. I barely know the place. What do you want to do?"

"Beats me. I guess we could go back to the hotel. There's a pool?"

Instead of trying to explain that fifteen-year-old girls don't hang out in hotel pools with their fathers, I just say: "I didn't bring a suit and I am not going back inside now that we finally made our break."

He three-point turns the car and heads out the driveway.

"What do you and Zach normally do for fun?" he asks in a way that implies we do stuff we shouldn't, but I ignore his tone.

"Well, normally we ride the school bus or play video games. Three times we've ridden bikes together — twice at night — over to your father's house. Once we explored a cave and found my dead uncle and his friend. You maybe wanna do something like that?"

He glances over at me and rolls his eyes. "I always forget how sarcastic you are in person. Did you eat lunch?"

"Yep. My mom's a chef. I never miss a meal. You?"

He nods and drums his fingers on the steering wheel to show that his patience is waning.

"Okay. I have an idea," I suggest reluctantly.

He glances over, then back at the road, and waits.

"Show me the gravel pit."

"The what?"

"Mom says she used to swim in a gravel pit but Zach says he's never heard of one around here. So I'm just, you know, curious about where it is."

"Like the gravel pit where the car James and Luke were

driving was found?" He gives me that knowing look so I stare back, deadpan. He's not getting anything on me.

"They were last seen in a gravel pit but ended up in a cave on your father's property?" I ask, trying to sound genuinely surprised.

He shifts in his seat, stares hard at the road, then turns on the radio. Static fills the car, followed by a blast of country music. He turns it off again. We share a distaste for country music. Perhaps it's genetic.

"Okay. I'll show you the gravel pit," he says and turns down a side road. "But promise me — *on your life* — that you'll never, *ever* tell your mother I took you there."

"Cross my heart."

✗ ✗ ✗

It takes some time to find a place to pull off the road, but eventually Dad finds an overgrown lane, puts the car in park, and opens the door. I climb out of the passenger side and look around at a wall of trees. For some reason I was expecting more dirt — or at least more gravel — and less foliage. Every time I leave the house lately, it seems I end up in the middle of a forest.

"You're sure this is the right place?" I ask skeptically.

"Yep. We have to walk down this lane a couple of minutes. From the looks of it, they don't use this pit anymore."

"Maybe because it's a crime scene?"

"Or maybe they exhausted all the sand and gravel."

The further we walk, the narrower the lane becomes, until we're pushing back branches and sidestepping raspberry canes. I'm at least wearing running shoes and jeans but Dad is in sandals and cargo shorts. *Rookie mistake*, I think to myself. Eventually we come to the edge of what was once a steep, sandy incline. It's overgrown with shrubs and saplings, but between the roots and dead leaves, sand is still visible.

"Wow. This is so weird," he says. "I didn't expect it would be overgrown like this. In my mind I just always pictured it the way it was the last time I was here."

"Which was when?"

"The day before the boys went missing. Your mother and I came down for a swim."

We scramble down the side of the pit and wind our way through mounds of overgrown gravel. Eventually we find ourselves on the edge of a pool of water, stagnant and brown, thick with algae, the surface alive with skittering bugs.

"You used to swim here?"

"Back then the water was beautiful. Clear and turquoise. There were several pools so watch where you walk."

I step sideways and a frog hops into the water, making concentric circles ripple across the surface. A few feet away, his little green face surfaces through the algae-thick water and he hangs motionless, staring back at me with what feels like reproach. I'm not a big fan of reptiles or amphibians and the blank-eyed stare isn't helping endear him to me. I pull out my phone to capture a bit of the frog, then pan out to include a shot of my father staring down at the water.

"Did you see James and Luke that day?"

"We saw James. He came down when we were swimming. I never met Luke." He pauses, shifts his feet. "Not properly, you know. Just saw him around a couple times. He hadn't lived here very long."

We walk along the bank of the pool. It's not an easy task. One of us is either pushing back a branch or stepping over a boulder. But we make our way to the far side where another pool comes into view. This one is less overgrown and the water is more blue than brown. But it's still not somewhere I'd ever consider swimming.

Dad looks around as if still trying to get his bearings. "I think this is the one where we used to swim. We were probably lying right here on our towels when James showed up."

"What did he want?"

"Nothing. He hung out for a bit, went for a swim, did some cannonballs, then took off. We stayed another hour or so and then went home."

He leans on a boulder overlooking the pond and I climb up to sit with my legs hanging over the sides. The warmth of the sun trapped inside the rock seeps into the back of my legs. The burn feels good, grounds me, helps anchor me to the moment.

"But seriously, if this is where the car was found and they were driving it, how do you think they ended up at your place?"

I watch his expression, but he turns and saunters toward a third pool of water, and I have to scramble down from the boulder to catch up.

"Beats me. I guess if we knew that, we'd also know who was responsible."

"So you think it's unlikely they fell into that cave and, like, died of head traumas or something?"

His expression changes, quickly. I can't tell if it's guilt or fear but I get the sense he knows more than he's willing to admit — to me or to anyone.

"I guess I just assumed someone did something to them. The police certainly let on like they were looking for evidence of foul play, the way they turned your mother's farm upside down."

I have to give him points for a quick recovery. His shoulders relax again and he smiles at me warmly. He stretches his arms wide and turns in a half circle.

"This is the infamous gravel pit. What do you think?"

I look over my shoulder then back at my father. "To be honest, it's a bit of a disappointment."

"Yeah, sorry about that. But it was your idea. Don't forget I voted for swimming at the hotel."

We climb up the far side of the pit. There are fewer trees so we can see across the wide depression to where the roof of a house is visible.

"Let me get this straight. You and Mom were down here swimming and James showed up and he went swimming with you. Then he left and you never saw him again?"

He nods. "Pretty much. Your mom saw him again, of course. But, uh, I didn't. I hardly even saw your mother after that. I mean, when we were teenagers. My dad woke me up the next morning all freaked out and told me James was missing and we went over to help look for him. The place was swarming with cops and your mother was hysterical. I could barely talk to her. We all had to give statements to the police." He pauses and sighs. "Nothing was the same after that." Another pause. "I think about those boys every day."

✗ ✗ ✗

After the gravel pit, Dad drives us around town, pointing out different landmarks and relating them to tenuous memories of him and Mom: the covered bandstand at the park where they got caught in the rain after a movie and sat smoking cigarettes; the Dairy Queen where Mom worked and Dad spent hours on the sidewalk waiting for her shift to end; the diner (now a hairstylist) where they would go and drink coffee just to get the jitters and then stay up late talking; the arena where they went roller-skating.

"It's funny how much you remember about this place considering you didn't really live here. Mom never tells me anything. I'm not even sure she remembers being here."

"Then why did you come back?" he asks as he continues his tour of the main street of Hicksville.

"To be honest, I was being, well, a pain in the ass and skipping school." I pause, then decide I might as well come completely clean. "And sneaking out at night to film urbex videos."

"What kind of videos?"

"*Urban exploration.* It's a whole thing. You go out at night and explore abandoned places and film your experience."

"Sounds kind of dangerous," he says carefully. "And illegal?"

"Well, I guess. But the places are already abandoned and lots of people do it. So it's not like I'm hurting anything. I have my own channel on YouTube. One of my videos has twenty-six thousand hits."

I know he's not going to understand how hard it is to get that many hits on a video. I admit it might be a bit dangerous, but it could help me get into film school and I've started making money too. Not a lot of money, just a few hundred dollars. But if I can land a few more hits and find a way to do it ethically, whatever that might mean, who knows where I might end up.

"So that's it? Skipping school and making YouTube videos?" He raises his eyebrows and tilts his head to the side to let me know he thinks there's more to the story.

I take a deep breath. "There was one incident involving the cops. But my friend totally set me up."

He looks at me skeptically but doesn't say a word and I feel compelled to keep talking.

"Seriously, she just wanted to get me in trouble to get me out of the way. She likes my boyfriend."

He doesn't react right away, which is a relief, and I think maybe he's someone I could confide in more often. Eventually he says: "Did it work? Did she end up with your boyfriend?"

"I'm not sure. Maybe. Probably?"

"He can't be much of a boyfriend if he fell for a stunt like that. You're probably better off with Zach."

I feel the blood race up my neck and spread across my face as fast as an oil spill on water and I turn to look out the window. After a minute, I clear my throat. "I guess Mom didn't have any other options for a change of scenery."

I dare to glance over at him right when he's doing the same, which means our eyes meet accidentally. It's an awkward moment that we try to smile through to make it seem more normal.

"So now what? You want to get a coffee or something?" he asks finally and looks away, around at the stores on either side of the street as if he is looking for a particular place.

"I think you're supposed to suggest ice cream. There's a place by the train station."

Dad pulls a U-turn and heads back toward the train station. When I point out the ice-cream parlor, he laughs.

"That used to be the bowling alley. We used to go sometimes

on Friday nights. The place would be crawling with kids."

"Fun times in Hicksville, huh?"

"It *was* fun at the time. Maybe not what you're used to with FPS games and social media."

"FPS games?" I ask, surprised by the reference.

"I'm not as stuck in the dark ages as you think. Besides, Theresa's a bit obsessed with *Call of Duty*."

I think of asking exactly how old Theresa is but keep the question to myself and we finish the drive to the ice-cream parlor in silence. It's a noticeable gap that goes on too long and it makes me feel uncomfortable again. When we get to the front door, I hesitate. I'm not sure if I should walk inside first or if I should let him open the door for me. But before it gets too weird, he reaches around me and pushes the door open. The cold air hits us in the face and I shiver.

There are forty-two flavors of ice cream to choose from, but if you ask me, some of them are pretty repetitive. Chocolate peanut butter fudge and chocolate peanut butter cup look so similar, I wonder if they made a mistake and put out two pails of the same flavor. But I don't challenge the kid behind the counter, who looks uncomfortable just taking our order in the first place.

When we have our cones, we walk up the street to where the Colossus restaurant sits empty.

"This is where Mom's opening her restaurant. Apparently, the locals didn't love Greek food."

"Nice." He nods approvingly and licks his ice cream right at the cone to stop it from melting down his hand.

"So have you gone back to the house?" I ask to fill the next gap in the conversation. "Like inside?"

He shakes his head. "I don't have a key anymore. I doubt he kept a spare outside."

"Have you even looked in the windows?"

"No, have you?"

"Actually," I say, extending the last syllable. "I did look in the window, the day Zach and I went over to meet him."

I can feel the tension building in his shoulders, in the set of his jaw. He licks at his ice cream a little too aggressively and I take a deep breath. *Do I tell him what I saw? Do I show him the video I took? Will it make him feel better or worse knowing his face is plastered across the living room walls of that house?*

"And?" he says finally.

"It was outdated. But tidy. I guess I didn't expect that from a long-time bachelor."

Mitch rolls his eyes. "He was fastidious. Obsessed with things being in their place."

I notice he talks about his father in the past tense, as if the man was already dead, and I decide he probably doesn't need to see the footage I took.

"He has a laptop," I say, hoping to lighten the mood.

Mitch doesn't react to this bit of information at first and I lick my cone to keep myself from saying anything I shouldn't. I try to think how I'd feel if I was coming back to a place that held so many bad memories, coming back after so many years. *Why did he really come back?* I wonder.

Finally, he pops the last of the cone into his mouth and swallows. "Now that *is* a surprise."

"Maybe you should go have a look," I suggest. "You might find something interesting."

"Anything in particular you have in mind?"

"Pictures of you. A whole wall."

"My school photos?" he asks, then sniffs and shakes his head in disbelief. "I can't believe he left those up."

He buries his hands in his front pockets and watches the sidewalk for the next block. I finish my cone and think about turning us back. We're almost at the end of the main street, and after that it's a few blocks of houses, and after that it's farm fields. But I'm reluctant to intrude on his reverie so I slow my pace and notice he slows his in response. Eventually he stops altogether and turns around as if he's suddenly noticed he's no longer in Australia. We cross the street and head back the other side, without having to discuss the decision. It's automatic. And surprising. *Maybe we're more connected than I realize*, I think. Then I scold myself for pretending we have one of those close-knit father-daughter relationships like you see on TV.

"What was your father doing the night the boys disappeared?" I blurt out suddenly when we're halfway back to the car. It's like the words have been inside me all day, expanding, waiting to bubble out like one of those kids' science experiments where you add baking soda to vinegar. I'm the model volcano, spewing words like fake lava.

"My God. You're really obsessed with this, aren't you?"

"To be fair, it's not every day you find out your uncle was a missing kid and both your grandfathers are considered suspects."

"Point taken. But I have no idea what he was doing. I didn't keep track of him and it was before cell phones. The less I saw of him, the better." He pauses, then adds, "He was around the place somewhere."

"What were *you* doing?"

"Not much. I had a friend up with me that week. We probably just shot some pool and watched TV."

"Did he help search the next day too? When you and your dad went over to Mom's?"

My father scratches the stubble on his chin and coughs. He looks over his shoulder and flips the hair out of his face. It's obvious he's feeling uncomfortable but I don't interrupt or give him an out. I'm certain he knows more than he's letting on. He starts and stalls twice, then finally says, "I think so. At least I don't think he'd left yet. To be honest, I can't really remember. It was a long time ago."

He unlocks the rental car as we approach. I climb in quickly and watch him as he puts on his seat belt and checks his mirrors. His movements are self-conscious, measured, like he knows I'm watching and he's trying to keep his cool. A good daughter would back off for a bit, give him some breathing space, but there's no way I'm going to miss an opportunity to uncover evidence, that one minuscule clue that clicks into place and allows all the other pieces to slide into order.

"Are you going to go see your father?"

His jaw tenses again and he grips the steering wheel tightly. He backs out of the parking space too fast and has to brake hard to miss the bumper of a black pickup truck.

"Geez, Kate. I don't know. I haven't spoken to him in over two decades. He's an asshole, and the last time I *did* see him I vowed I'd never talk to him again. Enough of the twenty questions."

The air in the car hangs heavy and I put down my window to let out some of the tension. I stare at the fields as we drive and, with relief, recognize that we're heading home. In hindsight, I regret that I've soured the mood.

"I'm sorry," he says quietly when the silence gets too thick for him. "I didn't mean to raise my voice. Of course you're curious. I would be too if I were you."

I shrug. "It's okay." But I keep my head turned away from him to let him know it's *not* okay. Even if I was pushing too hard, he shouldn't have yelled.

The tension continues to build like storm clouds inside the car until he pulls to the side of the road and turns off the ignition.

"What else do you want to know? You obviously have some questions you need answers to, so go ahead. Ask me anything."

"Why didn't you come back all this time?"

He pulls a long breath into his lungs then lets it go in a giant whoosh, but he doesn't speak. He stares out the window at the grassy field, then glances up at the sky where an airplane is tracking overhead. A car swooshes by and I wonder if we're parked in the safest place but I refuse to bring that up now. I want to know so badly I can feel the excitement rising in the back of my throat.

"The last time we saw each other, we had a fight," he finally says, slowly, and stops.

That's it? I wonder. *That's the whole explanation? If I left home because I had a fight with Mom …* But I don't say it. I know a fight with my mother is not in the same class as a fight with his father. But then he clears his throat and continues.

"It was a big fight. I confronted him about something I couldn't ignore any longer. And he threatened me. He threatened to hurt your mother. He blamed me for things I had nothing to do with. It was a terrible argument. Probably our first. But only because it was the first time I'd ever spoken up for myself."

The look on his face is fragile, as if the memory of his father, the last time he saw his father, is too much to recall, like I've broken him by asking him to remember. And I feel bad.

"Listen," he continues again. "I didn't know that was going to be the last time I saw him. I didn't mean to never come back. It's just, the longer I stayed away, the harder it was to come back. And so I just didn't. Until now."

I watch out the side window and consider his explanation.

The next time I turn to look at him, he seems calm and relaxed again. His hands are resting in his lap, and I feel stupid for suspecting my own father could somehow be involved in murdering two kids, especially since he was only a teenager himself. But the doubt won't leave me alone, won't let go of the thoughts in my head. It's insidious, like an echo in the recess of my dark imagination. *Just ask*, I tell myself. *Just ask and see what he does.*

"Okay. What were you doing in the drive shed last night?"

He laughs and glances up at the rearview mirror. A slight blush travels up his neck.

"I was looking for … my car."

"Your car?"

"When I left home, I had a car, and I wondered if it was still there. It's stupid. Of course he wouldn't have kept it. He probably sold it the day I took off. But I guess I sort of hoped it would still be there."

"What kind of car?"

"A 1976 Dodge Charger Daytona."

Dodge Charger? I think, and run the item through the database of my brain, trying to remember where I heard this recently. *When did I talk about old-fashioned cars?* I wonder. *Was it with Zach? Mom? Was it something I read?* Then it hits me.

"That's weird. Mom said James's favorite car was a Charger."

"I think it was everyone's favorite car back then. Dad got it for my sixteenth birthday. It was used but I loved it more than anything."

"I thought he was an asshole and yet he bought you a car?"

"Yeah, funny that. But it turns out he just wanted to have something he could take away from me."

"He wanted to control you?"

He swallows. "Exactly."

✗ ✗ ✗

When Mitch drops me back at the house, he doesn't turn off the engine. He leans over for a quick hug.

"Tell your mom hi for me and I'll text you later."

"You sure you don't want to come in for a coffee or something to make you jittery?" I tease, trying to lighten the mood again and, now that our afternoon is coming to a close, wishing I'd spent more time being chill and less time playing detective.

"I'm sorry but I need to have a nap. Still on Australia time. And I promised to FaceTime Theresa. Besides, being back here is a bit heavy after all these years. I could use a drink."

I close the car door gently and wave him off, then go inside. Mom is sitting at the kitchen table with her laptop, scraps of paper, and a notepad in front of her.

"Did you have a nice afternoon with your father?" She looks up casually, like she just noticed me there and hadn't heard the car pull up, like she wasn't counting the seconds until I returned.

"Yep. Pretty good. He took me for a drive around town and showed me all the landmarks from when you guys dated."

Mom's eyebrows shoot up with alarm. "He didn't!"

"Chill. I don't think he showed me whatever you're worried about."

She straightens the papers on the table in front of her, closes her laptop, takes off her reading glasses.

"I'm glad you had a nice time but be careful you don't get too attached. He's never been someone you could count on in an emergency."

I stand dead still and stare at her for so long, she looks down and starts to flip through the pages in her notebook.

"Why would you even say something like that? Are you jealous that I just spent four hours with my father? Four hours in two years?" I don't wait for a reply. Instead, I turn and stomp up the stairs.

Her reply is quiet but audible, and it follows me to my room, sneaks through before I close the door. "I just don't want you to get hurt like I did."

ZACH 10

Sunday morning arrives with a blast of cool air and the sound of Dad knocking on my door. I don't know if he's in a bad mood or has been knocking for a while, but it's a pretty aggressive tempo.

"Zach?" he says, cracking open the door to peer into my dark, cool room.

I sit up in bed and yawn. "What's up?"

"Just want to be sure you're still breathing. It's almost noon."

I pick up my phone to see if he's trying to pull a fast one, but he's not. The screen shows 11:48 a.m. and that I've missed several text messages. One from Josh and six from Kate.

"Also, Kate has been trying to reach you," Dad says.

I rub my eyes. "I can see that. But how do *you* know?"

"She's downstairs."

Dad turns and thumps back down the stairs before I can ask any questions. I jump out of bed and pull on a pair of jeans, almost in the same motion. Then I find a T-shirt on the floor that doesn't smell too bad and pull that on as well. I check my hair in the mirror — it's messy but passable. At least it looks clean.

I pocket my phone, then stop by the bathroom to throw water over my face and scrape a toothbrush around my mouth. All in all, it's less than five minutes before I land at the bottom of the stairs and Kate turns in her seat to smile and say good morning. As usual, my heart does a panicky little flip-flop in response. *Is that ever going to go away?*

"What's going on?" I ask and pull up a chair beside her. Dad has obviously cleared off part of the table, or more accurately, he's shifted a pile of junk to the far end to make room for a pot of coffee, the pitcher of milk, and the sugar bowl. Kate is holding a mug as if she needs to warm her hands.

"Not much. I tried texting but you didn't respond. So I was just talking to your dad."

I look from Kate to Dad to see if I've missed anything or if I should be nervous. "What were you talking about?"

"I was asking when they expect the forensic report and DNA results to come back."

She smiles and sips her coffee. I watch to see her reaction to the coffee, like if she's going to spit it back into the mug. Dad makes his coffee so strong it's been compared to motor oil by more than one person. But she doesn't flinch. In fact, she leans over and pulls a plastic container from her backpack.

"Mom sent over some muffins. Pumpkin spice and cream cheese in preparation for Thanksgiving."

She hands me the container. The muffins are still warm. I take one immediately and shove the crispy top into my mouth. It's delicious: moist and sweet like a dessert but with a secret spicy twist that makes me want ten more. Seriously. Is there nothing Sally can't make that tastes better than my expectations? I'm starting on my second muffin when I notice the room has gone quiet. I look up to see Dad and Kate staring at me, questions suspended in their expressions.

"What?" I ask as I shove the other half of the muffin in my mouth.

"Mom's going to take us into town for the afternoon," Kate says.

She stares at me without emotion, which I know by now is a sure sign that she's flipping her shit on the inside. I glance over at Dad, who looks impatient. He starts to clear the table.

"Oh, I get it," I say and lean back in my chair.

Dad shoots me a warning look that says: *Don't start something you can't finish.*

"You want us out of the way. You're worried we're going to interfere in the case again. One little mistake and we get banished."

Dad puts the mugs in the dishwasher and closes the door in slow motion, to match my own deliberate movements.

"Something like that, Zach. Grab whatever you need for the afternoon. Sally's going to drop you off at the mini-putt."

"Mini-putt? Do you think we're twelve?"

"Zach! You and Josh went mini-putting in June. I don't think you've outgrown it since then."

Kate clears her throat and shifts her gaze up and to the right. It's a small signal but I catch on.

"What?" I ask again, still annoyed that my day has been planned without my input.

"Mitch is picking us up and bringing us home after," Kate says matter-of-factly. She's obviously had longer to get used to the news.

"Why can't we just hang out here?"

Dad looks openly skeptical and Kate glances down at her knees.

"It's not like we're going to break into the dining room and start rifling through the cold case files." I hold three fingers up by my face. "Scout's honor."

"Nice try. You were never a scout."

"And we aren't going to sneak back to Peter Goheen's."

"That's true. You're not going back there," he says.

"We could hang out at Kate's?" I suggest and look at Kate who nods agreeably.

He sighs and sharpens his tone. "Just get your things. Sally will be here in a few minutes."

I roll my eyes at Kate but go get my jacket. On my way past, Dad hands me two twenty-dollar bills, kind of on the down-low. Then he says quietly, "This will be enough for a few rounds and lunch for you both." And then a bit louder, "Mitch will pick you up at four at the Colossus."

Dad shuffles Kate and I outside and we sit on the deck waiting for her mother to arrive.

"Don't feel bad. She woke me up at nine and dropped me off like I was going to day care."

"When did they hatch this plan?"

"Beats me. Apparently, Mom has to go meet with her lawyer. Something about her parents' estate."

"On a Sunday?"

"That's the story."

× × ×

The mini-putt is zoo themed, meaning there are fake animals and cages everywhere. It's been exactly the same since I can remember, and although I thought it was really cool when I was eight, seeing it now, through Kate's eyes, embarrasses me.

We carry our clubs and colored balls to the first hole. There's a painting of an elephant on the side of the building beside the tee and the ground is painted to look like a watering hole. A mother and two little boys are a few holes ahead and clearly having the time of their lives. Well, at least the kids are having fun. The mom looks pretty worn out.

"You any good at this?" I ask as Kate lines up her first putt.

"Not bad," she says and gets a hole in one.

"Not bad?"

"That was totally random." She throws back her head and laughs. "I almost never do that."

I roll my eyes. It takes me three putts to get my red ball in the first hole, which is typical.

We make our way through the first five holes behind the mother and two little boys, slowing our pace to let them move ahead. The boys argue and wrestle and ask five hundred questions. Their seven-year-old enthusiasm drains what little energy I have. It seems to be affecting Kate too. She's quieter than usual, withdrawn. I pull out my phone to see it's only 1:30 p.m. We still have two and a half hours to kill.

"Did you have a nice day with your dad yesterday?"

She nods and heads to the sixth hole, which is alligator themed. The ball has to travel along the tail, up the back of the alligator, then drop through a hole in its head and come out of its mouth. It takes Kate a couple of tries to get her aim lined up. Technically it's cheating, but I don't care.

"I guess. It was kinda weird. He took me to the gravel pit. Don't tell your dad. Or my mom."

"Seriously?"

She nods.

"Did he tell you anything interesting? Like why he was in the drive shed the other night?"

"He said he was looking for his car. Hoped his father hadn't sold it when he left home."

"And you believe him?"

She shrugs. "I did at the time. But now I think it was a red herring. Like, why didn't he take it with him? He said he loved that car. Why would he leave it behind if he loved it that much? Why would he come back looking for it all these years later. Like, from *Australia*?"

"Maybe you should ask your mom about the car."

Kate narrows her eyebrows. "What about it?"

"Just if she remembers it or whatever."

I get my ball to roll up the alligator's back on my second try, which puts me ahead, even with Kate's lucky hole in one. But technically we aren't keeping score and move on to the wombat hole.

"So anyway, I messaged CJ Grover on Facebook about the carving in the drive shed. Just to see if he'll respond," Kate says indifferently as she lines up and hits her ball.

"What did you say?" I ask, surprised she's acting so casual about something I consider fairly important news.

She shrugs and tilts her head. "I just said I noticed he'd commented on the aerial pictures of the Goheen property and asked what made him suggest the drive shed. It was pretty casual."

"Did he respond?"

She shakes her head. "Not yet."

"Maybe we should tell your dad about the carving and see how he reacts," I suggest.

Kate weighs this idea in her mind. "Maybe. When we were at the gravel pit, I felt sure he wanted to tell me something. Like, I think he knows more than he's letting on." She pauses and her tone becomes more somber. "Or he's hiding something. Or avoiding telling me something."

"Like what?"

"I don't know. But something."

"Wait a second! Maybe your dad is CJ Grover?"

Kate pauses to consider this while I buzz with the excitement of having connected enough random dots to arrive at such an astute conclusion. I mean, it makes sense. He's connected to the case, has an interest in the drive shed, and is obviously trying to hide something.

"But why would he pretend to be someone else?" she asks. Her brain works so quickly, I'm once again reminded that I have to be on top of my game to stay anywhere near her.

"I don't know, but think about it. Maybe he wants the case solved but doesn't want to be directly involved." I deflate a bit while I ponder the possibility that my brilliant deduction might not be so brilliant after all.

"I dunno." Kate backtracks. "It was just a gut instinct. I could be way off base. Maybe he knows nothing. Maybe he was just acting weird because it's weird to be back here and seeing me after two years. And seeing me here especially."

"But still, it makes sense," I say. "Why else would he fly from Australia so suddenly, and without letting you know? It doesn't really add up. Unless he's here for another reason. To hide something. Or to make sure something isn't found. Or to make sure something *is* found."

She drums her club against the ground and looks up at the sky. There are three seagulls circling overhead and I think: *They're a long way from home.*

"Do you think he made the carving?" Kate asks.

"I don't know what your dad is up to but I do know one thing," I say.

"What?"

"We need to tell *my* dad what we found."

I've been anxious about this for two days and I can feel the pressure building in my chest. Dad would tear a proverbial strip off me if he knew I had important information I wasn't sharing with him. And I know it's important, that any little thing can be the clue that breaks a case. I look at Kate while she ponders my suggestion and the conflict flutters at my throat.

"No. Not yet. Give me a couple of days to see what I can find out from Mitch. If I can get him talking, he might tell me more than he would the police. It could save time in the long run."

My anxiety surges, just a little, like the little burble of water before a geyser spews. "But it must be important. We're, like, withholding evidence or something. I don't know the exact term but I'm sure it's illegal. And my dad is gonna kill —"

Kate interrupts and by the tone of her voice I know she isn't going to budge. "Just give me a day. *One* day. Please? I need time to think. And maybe figure out what Mitch is hiding or knows. I mean, what if it implicates him somehow?"

Suddenly I realize that, as much as I'm feeling the pressure of being caught between Kate and my father, she's feeling her own kind of pressure. I mean, what if Mitch really *is* involved. I shiver at the thought. It's unlikely he harmed the boys but what if he's also been withholding evidence, or whatever. The last thing Kate needs is her father involved in this cold case too.

"Maybe that's why he left town so suddenly," I suggest quietly.

Kate lets her club hang loose at her side and sits down on a nearby bench. I wave a young couple ahead of us, then join her. I sit with my knees angled toward her but not touching. She stares at the ground so I can't see her expression, but she wipes her fingers under her eyes, quickly, like she's catching a tear before it can drop into her lap.

"I'm sorry. I didn't mean to suggest ..." I tap my club on the ground.

"It's okay. I mean, I've been thinking the same thing since he showed up in the drive shed. It's a good story about the car, but I don't quite buy it. You'd think that if you hadn't seen your kid in two years, that would be your first stop, not looking for a car from thirty years ago."

Silence envelops our bench. Even the little boys a few holes ahead have stopped squealing and showing off to one another.

"I'm sorry. If it makes you feel any better, my mom took off for a year and didn't even consider taking me."

Kate looks up and sighs. Her eyes are brimming with tears but she holds them back. "At least we have each other," she says. Then she smiles wryly, and the sad moment shifts like clouds moving past the sun. "Let's finish this game."

At the eleventh hole, Kate's phone vibrates and she pulls it from her back pocket.

My phone quacks like a duck, which is the ringtone I picked for an incoming message from Dad. I read the text, then look up at Kate. Our eyes meet and a zap of energy passes between us.

"Police station?" we say at the same time. Then, without a second thought about finishing our game, we head across town, our mini-putt clubs abandoned on the bench.

× × ×

Dad meets us at the front of the police station — a square, yellow-brick building moated by tarmac — when we show up, breathless from power walking the three miles. He escorts us through a maze of empty cubicles, through a darkened hallway, and into his brightly lit office where Sally is already sitting, leaning forward, her knees pressed tight together. Her eyes are red and she's holding a crumpled tissue in her hand.

Dad motions for us to sit down in the chairs beside Sally, while he sits in his on the opposite side of the desk.

"You got the forensic report back?" I ask finally, breaking the silence with an almost-whisper.

Sally sniffles and Dad nods. It's a slow, resigned nod, the kind of nod nothing good can follow.

"And?" Kate asks impatiently.

I swallow again, trying to eliminate the buildup of saliva in the bottom of my mouth, drowning my tongue. My heart starts to race and anxiety bubbles up like hot lava in my chest. I know there's no way to stop the geyser this time, definitely not with standard breathing exercises. Instead, I let my eyes wander around the room.

What are five things I can see? I ask myself, then count them off on my fingers: the taupe-colored wall, the wood grain in the desk, the blue-flecked carpet, Kate's knee jiggling with nervous energy, the pen in Dad's hand. He's tapping it against a plastic desk protector.

"You know I can't share much. But I can tell you what I've already told your mother. The report shows trauma to both sets of remains. One of the deceased suffered worse than the other. Broken legs, broken ribs, a fractured pelvis. All that occurred at or around the time of death. It's impossible to know for sure. The other had a gunshot wound to the back of the skull."

Sally inhales sharply, holds her breath, wipes at her eyes with the soggy tissue.

My heart lurches again and my pulse is like a drumbeat in my temples. I feel like my chest might burst wide open.

What are four things I can feel? I ask myself and let my fingers run over the fabric of my jeans and the vinyl upholstered chair. I feel my hair brush the skin on my neck and a vent from above blowing cold air on the crown of my head. I take a series of long, slow, deep breaths. I haven't had a full-blown panic attack since Kate showed up in my life. Even though they are largely unpredictable, I had my first serious one the day Mom moved out of the house.

"A gunshot wound?" Kate mouths. She appears rattled by this information and I know she's remembering the day we met Peter Goheen.

Three things I can smell, I prompt myself: coffee in Dad's mug, the faint vanilla scent of Kate's hair, a box of dusty files by the door.

"Did Mitch have a gun?"

Sally startles when Kate uses *Mitch* instead of *Dad*, but she doesn't call her on it. "I think so. Yes. I'm pretty sure he had a .22."

"There was a bullet recovered at the scene that might help us narrow the search, but it still doesn't give us much to go on," Dad says, bringing us all back to reality.

Two things I can hear: my racing heart, Sally blowing her nose.

It suddenly feels as if the air has been sucked out of the room.

"But at least we have a lead now, right? We've been waiting thirty-five years for a break in this case," Sally says, then gulps back a big breath of air and stutters: "I just don't know that I can go through it all again."

Kate leans into her mother, and they hold on to one another like life rafts, each sustaining the other in turns.

One thing I can taste: Sally's despair.

KATE 10

The Colossus is six blocks from the high school so I walk up at the end of the day Monday to help Mom clean, paint, and generally get the place open for business. When I arrive, she's in the kitchen standing on the stainless-steel counter, wiping down the exhaust fan with disinfectant.

"So this is it, huh?"

I drop my backpack on a chair and watch her from the floor: she scrubs, dunks her hand in the bucket of soapy water, wrings out the rag, repeats.

"Yes. This is all ours for one year. With an option to lease at the same rate for a second year."

"How long do you think it'll take to get the place ready?"

"A week."

"A week?"

"Yep. The Grand Opening is in two weeks. But don't worry. It won't take long to pull things together. Other than being dirty, the kitchen is perfect. And I have the menu set."

I look into the main room. There're stacks of tables and chairs piled in the corner. The floor is thick with the dirt and debris from past renovations, the windows are covered with yellowed newspapers, and the walls are covered in hand-painted murals of what I can only assume are scenes from rural Greece.

"Stop fretting. I've done this before, remember?" Mom says, then hops down from the counter and wipes a strand of hair behind her ear. She's wearing bright blue rubber gloves.

I do remember. Twice before Mom has taken an empty husk of a restaurant and turned it into a trendy, bustling bistro within the span of a month. And this place is by far the smallest.

"Do you have a name?"

"I'm thinking something straightforward. Not too fancy. Like 'Sally's Sweet Eats.'"

"Sweet?"

"I'm thinking of having a different flavor of homemade gelato every week."

She pauses to watch my expression so I smile and say, "Cute." Then I nod at her gloved hands and add, "What about The Scullery Maid?"

Mom scowls but doesn't respond. Instead, she tosses me the broom.

"The Prodigal Daughter?"

Mom ignores my smirking. "Maybe something less biblical."

I take the broom to the front corner of the dining room and work my way toward the back, sweeping a larger and larger mound of dirt and debris ahead of me.

"I just thought it would be good to address it head on, you know, that you're back in town," I explain after a few minutes of sweeping. "Everyone's probably already gossiping about you being back anyway."

"I'll think about it," Mom says brightly, then dumps the bucket of water down the slop sink by the back door. She refills the pail and starts wiping down the lower shelves.

When I finish sweeping, Mom puts me on cleaning windows. It takes half an hour just to peel off the three-year-old newspapers and scrape away the baked-on masking tape.

"Remember you said James's dream car was a Dodge Charger?" I call from where I'm spraying window cleaner and wiping black grime onto paper towels.

She steps out from the kitchen and watches me. "Yeah."

"Turns out Mitch had a Dodge Charger. A Daytona."

"That's right," Mom says, a little too wistfully for my liking.

"Did James like Mitch's car? Like, was he crazy about it or something?"

"Everyone liked Mitch's car. Back then most of us were lucky to get to borrow our parents' pickup trucks once a week. Plus, his had a custom paint job. Burnt orange with yellow flames."

"Sounds fancy. He came back to look for it, you know?"

I pull a new handful of paper towel off the tube and stand on my tiptoes to reach the top corner of the window. A mother and her young daughter ride by on bikes. The mother nods and smiles at me through the freshly cleaned glass, and the girl wobbles down the sidewalk.

"You're kidding."

"Apparently. He went to the drive shed at his dad's but it was gone."

A strange look creeps over Mom's face, like she's trying to remember the secret ingredient in a favorite family recipe.

"I thought his father sold it. Like at the beginning of that summer. I remember how mad Mitch was. And me too. We had to borrow my mom's station wagon."

"You're sure?"

"I think so. Yeah. I remember a couple weeks before James disappeared we went to the drive-in — and we were definitely not in the Charger," she says.

"Mom!"

"Relax. My friend Jenn was with us. And your father's friend. I remember we spilled popcorn and Mom told me to vacuum the whole car the next day. But I paid James two bucks to do it."

"What friend of Mitch's?"

"I think his name was Tom. Or Todd? He was Italian anyway. And his first name started with a T?"

"The guy in the photo with you and James and the gun?"

"Yeah, that guy. I always forget his name."

"I think you said his name was Tony."

"Yes, that was him."

"Was he the same friend who came and helped search for the boys?"

Again, Mom scrolls through her memory. "I don't recall him being there during the searches. But I could have forgotten. There was so much chaos and I don't remember much," she says before she disappears back into the kitchen and turns on a tap.

I'm putting some extra elbow grease into a patch of stubborn tape adhesive when I see Zach and his dad walking across the street. Zach is carrying a picnic basket and his father is carrying a cooler. Zach looks decidedly uncomfortable, then blushes when he sees me watching.

I wave out the window, then put down my cleaning stuff to open the door.

"Hi!" I say and step aside to let them in. Then I call out: "Mom! We have company."

Zach's dad reddens slightly when Mom pops her head around

the kitchen doorframe, but Mom looks horrified to be seen in her cleaning outfit: ratty track pants, a baggy T-shirt, hair up in a messy bun.

"Welcome to Mom's new restaurant," I say to fill the silence.

Zach's dad looks around at the mess. "It's really coming together," he says with an inappropriate amount of enthusiasm.

I'm not sure how to respond. If I offer a reality check, it will seem rude. If I agree, I'll come across as insincere. Instead of making things worse, I stand in one spot and say nothing.

"Zach, maybe you can set up a couple of those tables," his father suggests.

Mom finally appears from the kitchen, still in her baggy T-shirt and 1990s track pants, but she's washed her face and let her hair down.

"The place has been empty for so long. It needed a good cleaning." She touches her hair to be sure it's still where she left it.

"Don't worry about that for now. We brought dinner for four!" Zach's dad says proudly and with the same level of enthusiasm as a kindergartener showing off his new bike.

"That's so considerate. Thank you."

I take this as my cue to help Zach with the table and chairs. He has them set up but I bring over my window cleaner and give them a good wipe down.

He leans in close, tilts his face toward the floor, and speaks under his breath. "Anything back from CJ Grover?"

I shake my head. "Not last I checked, which was about five minutes ago."

Zach and I unpack the picnic basket while Mom shows off the kitchen and I have to hand it to Zach and his dad. They've thought of everything: cutlery, cloth napkins, salt and pepper shakers, hot sauce, wine glasses, a corkscrew. We set up the table in the cleanest corner of the restaurant, just below the painting of an olive grove.

Finally, Mom and Zach's dad join us at the table. He pulls out a chair for Mom and then invites Zach and I to take a seat. He places soup bowls in front of us, then takes a pitcher from the cooler, which he's using as a hot box. *Clever*, I think to myself.

"Broccoli bisque!" he announces proudly as he fills each of our bowls. When he takes a seat, he pours himself and Mom a glass of wine. He has a bottle of lemon Perrier for Zach and me.

Mom is the first to take a tentative slurp of her soup. I watch carefully so I know what to expect. To my surprise, she smiles and says, "Yum. This is good." And I can tell she means it so I spoon some into my mouth too. Then I relax because somehow Zach's dad has managed to feed my mother something that doesn't make her screw up her face. She's a food snob. I rarely see her enjoy other people's cooking.

"It's vegan," Zach's dad announces with pride. "I used coconut milk instead of cream."

"Well, it tastes great. Zach never let on that you were such a great chef," Mom says graciously.

I feel my phone vibrate and sneak a look down at the text Zach has just sent me.

He's been cooking all day. He got up early.

I pocket my phone and shoot Zach a conspiratorial smile.

After the broccoli bisque, we have asparagus-stuffed chicken breast wrapped in prosciutto, with a side of rice pilaf and roasted root vegetables.

"Did you put saffron in the rice?" Mom asks after her first bite.

"I did!"

"It really works."

They banter back and forth about cooking while Zach and I clean our plates. When Mom's finished, she wipes her mouth and says, "If you ever decide to retire from the police force, I might have a job for you."

Zach's dad laughs loudly. "I don't know about that, but thank you. We wanted the first meal in your new restaurant to be a special one."

"We probably would have ordered pizza or something. But this was way nicer. Thank you very much."

"Have you decided on a name?" Zach asks, his first real contribution to the conversation since he arrived.

"She's still trying to come up with something? Got any ideas?"

"What about The Sally-vate Café?" Zach suggests.

Mom laughs.

"The Sally-mander Bistro?"

Mom scowls.

"Or how about Sal-acious?"

Zach is clearly on a roll with his puns.

Finally, Zach's dad clears his throat. "Mustang Sally's?"

A slow, nostalgic smile takes over Mom's face.

"Look at you! Bringing a gourmet dinner *and* coming up with a great name for my new place. Aren't you full of surprises?"

He shifts uncomfortably in his seat, and his mouth tightens, turning his smile into a grimace. "There's actually a second reason for our visit."

Mom's expression turns cold and the set of her shoulders hardens. The mood in the room changes, the temperature drops, the air becomes thick and hard to breathe. Dinner feels heavy in my stomach and I regret the second helping of rice. Zach averts his gaze and taps his fork on the rim of his plate. Everything is in slow motion. My chest is so tight I can barely inhale.

"We got the DNA results back this morning."

Mom doesn't dare look up. She stares down, past the edge of the table to her lap. I imagine her standing on a precipice with sharp drops on all sides. She has to take the next step but there's nowhere left to go but down the steep, rocky mountainside.

Zach's dad inhales, deeply, before continuing. "The remains with the more severe trauma — the fractured pelvis, broken ribs and legs — there's a direct match with Luke McLeod."

Mom sucks in her breath and holds it. I know what's scrolling through her head: James was the one who was shot and that's better. It was fast, he didn't suffer like Luke must have. But at the same time there's no more hope to drip feed from. The end of James's story has finally been revealed. I shift my gaze to Mom's face and read the emotions spooling there. They match my own: relief, grief, anger, sadness, resolve.

"There was something unusual though," Zach's dad continues.

Now Mom looks up from her lap to study his face. I do too. Zach is still looking away, past my shoulder and out the window. *He already knows what's coming,* I think, and try to glean some information from his expression. But he's impossible to read, his face a blank canvas. He's deliberately distancing himself from the news his father has to share. I know that. I just can't figure out why.

"Unfortunately, there's been no match for the second victim, the one with the gunshot wound. It didn't match your DNA, Sally."

The room becomes a vacuum, a black hole sucking awareness and comprehension beyond our grasp. Now the emotions reverse on Mom's face. Resolve gives way to confusion, then hope, then despair again.

"I don't understand," Mom whispers.

I grab on to the seat of my chair with both hands and hold on tight so I don't tumble headlong into the black hole as well. I look at Zach, hoping his eyes will anchor me, but he looks as lost as I feel.

"There's no chance you and James weren't actually related, is there?" Zach's father asks.

Mom looks confused. "No. No chance at all. He was definitely my brother. I remember them bringing him home from the hospital."

"I'm sure you're right. But what about you? You're sure you weren't, say, adopted or something? And nobody ever told you?"

"I can't see how. I mean, I've seen pictures of me with mom when I was a newborn. I remember her talking about being pregnant with me. Apparently, I caused her terrible morning sickness, which never happened with James." Mom shakes her head while she processes this information. "I know James and I were siblings, full siblings. I just know. If it wasn't true, my Aunt Kathy would have told me after Mom died."

"I didn't think so. Really. There's too much family resemblance to ignore, and even if you had different fathers, or if you'd been born to a relative or something like that, the DNA would still show a connection between you. That is, if the remains were James's." He pauses and runs his hand through his hair. "We're running the results against known databases, but so far there're no matches."

"But you found his wallet. With his student card?"

Zach's dad shakes his head sadly. "We're trying to figure that part out, but you know the boys were together when they were … last seen … so perhaps Luke had James's wallet? For some reason? Or the other person did?"

Mom thinks about this. I can almost see the mechanisms in her brain turning, her memory trying to rewind to the day she last saw her brother, if there was a reason why Luke might have had James's wallet.

Finally, she looks up at Zach's dad and stutters, "Do you think James is still alive?" She can barely finish speaking the word *alive* before she starts gasping. She stutters and grabs the cloth napkin from her lap to soak up the tears that have started to flow. "I'm sorry," she says. "Every time I see you, I end up crying."

Zach is looking at me when I glance back at him. There's recrimination in his expression. I can feel him urging me to bring up the carving in the drive shed but I can't. Not yet.

"We're going to Fort Erie tomorrow to meet with Mr. McLeod and share the news. Tell him what we've found. Mrs. McLeod passed away a few years back. But Luke's father is still alive. And his two siblings."

I try to imagine what it will be like for Mr. McLeod to learn Luke was dead all this time, his body lying in a cave so close to their home. How will he feel about James when he hears Luke wasn't with him at the very end? Will he resent my uncle somehow, blame him for not also being confirmed dead? Next, I glance at Mom and I wonder if she's wishing for the same closure the McLeods are finally going to get, whether she would gladly trade in hope for closure.

ZACH 11

Kate texts me the next morning before school. I'm not even out of bed yet but I roll over, unplug my phone, and squint at the words.

I have a new friend on Facebook!

I sit up in bed.

CJ Grover?

Yep.

My pulse races and my fingers fumble on the keypad.

*What's on his deed? *feed*

I lean back on a pile of pillows and wait for Kate's response. She's like the Lightning McQueen of texting though, so it doesn't take long.

Not much. Pics of some kids playing baseball. Some old people on a beach. Looked like Jamaica. Memes mocking Trump. Music videos from the '80s. The regular stuff of old people.

Did he message you back about the initials in the drive shed?

Nope. Just accepted my friend request so far.

I stand up and pace the room. I can't believe Kate isn't freaking out like I am. That girl has seriously steady nerves.

Message him again.

I WILL. GEESH. RELAX.

Now?

Yes. I just did. Back to waiting.

An idea flashes through my brain and I grab hold, trying not to get hung up on the consequences. My heart races and I feel a pressure building below my rib cage, like a two-hundred-pound gorilla lying across my chest. But I take a huge breath and funnel it through my nose to the count of eight. *Don't be predictable. Be spontaneous. Be interesting,* I tell myself. I look at my thumbs hovering above the keypad and will them to cooperate.

Wanna ditch today? I finally text.

And do what?

Research. Dad's gone to Fort Erie. He won't be back until dinner.

What do you want to research?

Missing people from 1982. Someone must know who the second guy is.

Be there after the bus goes past

I spring to action trying to make the house more present-able, and Kate arrives thirty minutes later looking nervous and glancing over her shoulder as though she's a serious criminal. She practically pushes me out of the way to get inside.

"Hi," I say sarcastically. "Come on in."

She looks around. "You cleaned up for me?"

"Nah," I lie, and look around with mock insult. "We do a big marathon clean every Sunday."

Kate peels off her jean jacket and hangs it on the back of a kitchen chair. Then she sits down. She stretches her legs out straight and lets her arms hang at her sides.

"Sorry. That was nerve-racking. Mom was still home when I left. I walked to the end of the driveway, then hid behind some bushes until the bus went by. Much easier to skip when you live in a city and can just melt into the crowds. How long until the school calls?"

I wipe toast crumbs off the table as I sit down, hoping she won't notice.

"Usually the end of the day," I say. "So that gives us a few hours. Maybe I'll get lucky and Dad'll still be gone when they call." I clear my throat and try to imitate Dad's voice: "Hello. Al Whitchurch here. Yes, Zach is home sick today. Sorry for not calling sooner."

Kate laughs. "Not bad if they've never spoken to your father."

"Can you do your mother? You could call the automated attendance line?"

Kate's eyes light up and she picks up her phone. She tries a few different voices before she dials and then watches me as she talks.

"Hi, this is Sally Cooper, Kate Cooper's mother. Kate is home sick today with strep throat. The poor thing. Her fever is skyrocketing. Please call me on my cell phone if you have any concerns about her keeping up with her schoolwork. Thanks."

When Kate hangs up, we both burst into laughter, that stomach-busting kind that goes on and on, and gets renewed by the slightest change in expression. Like, when she raises one eyebrow, I double over again. I'm laughing so hard it actually hurts my abs. But I'm not gonna lie, it also feels good to laugh. It's a relief. I can't believe how confidently she pulled that off. She didn't even flinch.

When I finally catch my breath, I say, "That might just work. But what if they call her cell phone?"

Kate wipes tears of laughter from her eyes. "This isn't my first rodeo. I put *my* cell phone number under *her* name when I filled out the emergency contact sheet."

That sets us off again on another, smaller bout of laughter. But when we sober it happens quickly, and we look around at reality closing in, looming above, staring us down.

"Okay, so we both ditched school, and despite that Oscar-level performance, I hate to tell you, but I'm going to get caught — which means you're going to be in for it too. First for ditching and then for impersonating your mother."

Kate shrugs. "Too late now. I'm sure by the end of the day there'll be a few more misdemeanors to add to the list."

I've already got my laptop open on the kitchen table. Kate leans over to see what search term I've entered and the tabs I have open.

"Anything promising?"

"I found a couple of cold case sites."

She pulls her chair close and we huddle together in front of the screen. I open, scan, and close pages as soon as I suspect a dead end. Finally, we land on a searchable missing person site that looks promising.

"The Doe Network. It covers the U.S., Canada, New Zealand, Mexico, Australia, and Europe."

I narrow my search by geography and gender until I'm staring at 126 photos of missing males.

"Maybe one of these faces belong to the unidentified skeleton," I say.

I scroll to the 1980s and see James and Luke listed side by side, their faces staring out optimistically at us, with so much potential and without a hint of the tragedy that is lurking in the shadows.

Kate leans in closer and examines the other faces. "What about that guy there? Anthony Frank Lomangino?"

She points to a young man on the row below James and Luke. His age is listed as twenty when he went missing in October 1982. His face is almost a profile and he's smirking, as if someone in the next frame just told an off-color joke. He has thick black hair, curly, wild, and unkempt. It looks like he could use a shave.

"But what would a twenty-year-old be doing with a couple of fifteen-year-olds?" I ask.

"I don't know. Maybe he was in the area for summer holidays and they, like, ran into each other in town?" Kate suggests.

I scowl.

"What are the circumstances of his disappearance?"

I open the page.

"It says he wasn't close to his parents but kept in touch with his sister. She hadn't seen him since June of that year but she wasn't sure of the exact date. His roommate said it wasn't unusual for him to be gone for a week or two at a time and had last seen him mid-August. He also wasn't sure of the exact date but possibly around the sixteenth. It wasn't until October when he was officially reported missing. He didn't show up at his sister's wedding, which apparently was odd, even for him."

"That's super sketchy. Did anyone try to find him?"

"It doesn't say. But the timing makes sense for our mystery guy. He might have been missing longer but nobody realized it."

"It says he's from Etobicoke. Where's that?" Kate asks.

"Near where your mom took us to shop for all that restaurant stuff."

Kate scowls and rolls her eyes. "Ah. Good times."

"It's probably not him, but I can at least show this to Dad when he gets home."

Kate gets up and paces while she thinks. She wanders toward the dining room and peers through the glass doors. The boxes of case files are stacked along the wall, the table covered in the folders Dad has been reviewing in the evenings and on weekends. She puts her hand on the doorknob.

"It's locked," I remind her.

"But what if there's something in those files that a fresh set of eyes …"

"No."

"He'll never find out if we're careful. If we just have a look and put everything back where we found it?"

"No."

Kate walks into the kitchen and takes a butter knife out of the sink. She wipes it on a tea towel and heads back to the dining room door.

"What are you doing?"

"I just want to see if I can pop the lock."

I hover by the door. "Have you done this before?"

She shoots me that look that says: *What do you think?*

"Don't wreck anything," I say. I'm not too worried about her getting in. I can't see the butter-knife method working.

"Relax."

She slides the knife between the door and the frame, flicks it down, and the lock pops. The door swings inward slightly, as if offering us an invitation to enter. Kate flashes me an *I-told-you-so* look, then pushes the door open and steps inside. I'm still trying to figure out how she did that when she walks around the table and reads the names on the folders that are lying in full view. I follow her, ready to put her in a choke hold if she so much as reaches out to touch a single piece of paper. She points at a folder and I swat her hand away.

"I'm not going to get us in trouble. *Relax*."

She leans over to get a closer look.

"This is a medical report about James. July 1982. I wonder why your dad was looking at this?"

"To see if any previous injuries matched the remains?" I suggest.

"So maybe the DNA results weren't a total surprise to him?"

I shrug and Kate keeps reading. She glances at me, then slowly reaches out to flip over a page of the report. I feel my stomach clench and my chest tighten but I don't stop her. I don't have it in me to disappoint her.

"This is terrible, Zach. He had four broken ribs, a fractured radius and ulna from a previous injury, and a broken clavicle. Plus, internal bleeding. He was in the hospital for two weeks."

I lean over to see what she's reading.

"His father did that to him. I can't believe they let him go home after that. Didn't they have, like, Children's Aid Societies back then?"

"I'm sure they did. But maybe they didn't know the whole story. Does it say what caused the injuries?"

Kate scans the report and flips the page. "Yeah. It says he crashed his friend's dirt bike. But didn't that article we read online, the one where they interviewed Mr. McLeod, didn't that say his dad beat him up and sent him to the hospital?"

I nod. "Obviously they lied to the doctors."

Kate takes out her phone and lines it up to take a picture but I block the report with my hand.

"No way. No photos. It's bad enough that you're in here looking."

She pockets her phone and moves around the table. She stops, reads, looks up at me. "Here's Mom's statement."

Together we read the account Sally gave of last seeing James and Luke in the gravel pit.

"This is very specific. She was drinking Grape Crush and reading *Cujo* when the boys showed up to drive her to her friend's house," Kate says. "Everything else is pretty much what she told me. It's weird though, hearing her as a teenager. And to think she remembers so little now."

Kate flips to the final page. "Look, Zach! Your father wrote this report. He must have interviewed my mom." She points to his signature and the date. "So they did meet before," she says softly.

Kate lifts the report to look below.

"Mitch's statement!"

She kneels on one of the chairs and picks up the report. I start to protest but she raises her hand to silence me. I pace behind her, my nerves raw. My heart starts to pound and I take several deep breaths to keep the anxiety from taking over. I peer out the window to be sure Dad isn't coming down the driveway, even though I know it's ridiculous. He's probably still on his way to Fort Erie.

"Kate. I really think you should ..."

Again, the hand.

Another four laps of the dining room.

"Check this out. Mitch's statement about the day he last saw James at the gravel pit — not the day they went missing but the day before — is the same as he told me the other day. But this part about going over to help search the day *after* the boys went missing — well, it's different."

"Different how?"

"He told me he had a friend over that weekend and they went together to help search. But here it says his friend went home the morning before the search."

Kate returns to her mother's statement and flips through the pages.

"Look. This is Mom's statement about the morning of the first search. She mentioned that Mitch and his dad came over to help look for the boys. But she didn't mention a friend at all."

She goes back to Mitch's statement. "He definitely said his friend left first thing that morning, then he and his dad went over to the Coopers' together."

"Does it say who the friend was? Is there a statement from him?"

Kate flips back a page of Mitch's statement. "Oh my God, Zach!"

My heart flips and my stomach tumbles. "What?"

"His friend was named Tony!"

I stare at Kate blankly.

"We were talking about Mitch's friend yesterday. Mom couldn't remember his name at first — said it started with a T — and that he was Italian. But then she was pretty sure it was Tony. I think we have a picture of him in our house. That's why he looks familiar!"

My brain starts buzzing like an electric bug zapper and I rush back to the laptop where the Doe Network is still open on the missing twenty-year-old man from Etobicoke.

"Anthony Frank Lomangino! Tony is Anthony!" I shout.

My heart races with excitement and fear and who knows what else. "We *have* to tell Dad," I say. "We have to come clean about the initials in the drive shed and this too. No more waiting."

My tone is stern, and in response, Kate's expression turns serious. She puts down the reports exactly as she found them, closes folders, backs out of the room, and locks the door behind her. She wipes down the butter knife as if she's worried about fingerprints and puts it in the drawer. If I didn't know her better, I'd think she was an accomplished burglar. She sits at the kitchen table for a moment, then takes a picture of Anthony Frank Lomangino's on-screen picture with her phone.

I grab my phone, trying to decide exactly what to say to my father and the best way to say it. I'm hoping Kate will help me but she seems suddenly restless. She stands up again.

"How long until your dad gets back?" she asks.

I shrug. "Like, maybe five hours?"

"Is it okay if I use your washroom?" she asks and heads off through the mudroom before I can even nod.

My mind is racing, trying to figure out what she's planning to do next. She didn't protest about telling my father and that alone makes me suspicious. When she returns to the kitchen, she has calculated resignation on her face.

"I think I'm going to go to school now," she says.

"Why? What about your strep throat?"

It's obvious her mind is on something else so I don't interrupt. I let her have time to think about what she wants to say next.

Finally, she says, "I think we cracked the case. Go ahead and text your dad or whatever you want. Or maybe it would be better to wait until he comes home and then you can tell him everything. About Anthony and the carving in the drive shed."

"You don't want to be here?" I ask.

"Not really. That's between you and him. I really think it's done. It's over. I'll just tell the school I'm feeling better now. That it was a false alarm, not strep."

"How are you going to get to school?"

"Mom'll drive me. I'll just tell her I missed the bus. Do you want to come too?"

The change in Kate's mood is so sudden and unexpected I don't know how to respond. I'm confused but I know I'm ten steps behind whatever she's planning. After running through the possibilities in my head, I eventually say, "No, that's okay. I'll hang out here. You can too if you want. We can play video games."

Kate shakes her head. "I'm feeling kind of bad about ditching. I'll text you later, okay? And I won't blow your cover. As far as I know you're already at school."

Before I can protest further, Kate picks up her jacket from the back of the chair and disappears out the back door.

KATE 11

Time slows down as I climb the hill home. For the first time in my life, I notice the texture of the pavement, the color of the stones that make up the gravel shoulder: pink, gray, black with shimmering flecks that twinkle in the sunlight. The air is thin and flows through my lungs effortlessly. My feet follow one another in a rhythmic pattern. The whole universe has shrunk to this one moment. Anyone who says time is a constant has never uncovered an unimaginable truth.

I step tentatively onto the front porch and swing open the door, pausing to listen for noises inside, clues about where my mother is in her day.

"Kate?" Mom calls out when the screen door slams shut. She appears from the living room, her purse in her hands and open as if she has been rummaging for something. She looks surprised to see me. Confused.

"What are you doing home? Did you miss the bus?" She looks at the time on her phone, scowls up at me. Then she glances past me, through the door, out to the driveway. No doubt she expects Mitch to appear, or Zach, or a police officer.

She steps forward, a quizzical look on her face. "Are you okay?"

"I'm okay. But we need to talk." I pull my phone out of my pocket and scroll to the photo of Anthony Frank Lomangino.

"Is this Mitch's friend? The guy you were telling me about that used to come and hang out with him sometimes on the weekend? The same guy in the picture with you and Mitch and James holding the gun?"

Mom takes the phone and looks carefully. She nods. "That's him. My God! He looks so young. Where did you find the picture?"

I swallow to dislodge the hard lump that is blocking my throat.

"On a missing person's website."

Mom opens her mouth as if she is planning to say something, but then she closes it again and just stares at me. The information is too random to process.

"He was reported missing in 1982. The fall. But his family hadn't seen him since June."

"He wasn't close to his family," Mom finally says. "I know he didn't live at home. I think he had an apartment in the city with some roommate." She pauses. "Yes. That's right. I remember Mitch sometimes stayed with him there, when he wasn't at school or up here."

Mom walks to the kitchen in a daze and I follow. We sit at the table across from one another and let the silence join us.

"What do you think this means?" Mom asks finally.

"I don't know. I don't want to jump to conclusions, but think about it. Two people close to Mitch go missing at the same time. Maybe not the exact same day, but the same time frame. That has to mean something."

Mom looks pale, like she might vomit. She puts her head in her hands and stares down at the table.

"Mitch wouldn't … He wasn't like his dad. He loved James," she says softly.

"Mom. I don't think he did anything to James either. Or to Luke. But he has to know something. The two cases *have* to be connected."

Mom nods but doesn't lift her head. She wipes a few crumbs off the table and onto the floor with one hand, drums her fingers on the table, continues to stare down.

"We have to talk to him. We have to tell him what we know and at least give him a chance to explain," I suggest gently.

She looks up with alarm. "When?"

"When he gets here."

Mom narrows her eyes at me. "Is he coming over?"

"I texted him and said I had something important to tell him."

× × ×

When we hear Mitch's car pull up outside, I go to the window and watch him open the car door, step out, take a deep breath. I wonder if his heart is pounding as hard as mine. Mom gets up and puts on the coffee while I go to greet my father.

"Hey," I say when he steps onto the porch.

"Hey back," he says, then searches my face.

"Come on in. I think Mom's making some coffee."

I turn and walk back inside with Mitch trailing. He kicks off his shoes and hangs his coat on a hook behind the door. I notice with irony that our three coats are lined up, shoulder to shoulder: his, Mom's, mine. It's the closest we will probably ever get to being a typical family.

Mom transfers the coffee pot and mugs to the table, pulls a

jug of cream out of the fridge, grabs the sugar bowl. Then she takes out a plate and transfers several cranberry muffins from a plastic container. She sets this down on the table too, along with some small yellow serving plates.

"Help yourself," she says as she sits down.

I rub my hands on my pant legs under the table. "We want to talk about Tony."

"Tony?"

"Your friend, Tony, from back then. His full name was Anthony Frank Lomangino."

Mitch nods slightly. His expression is impossible to read, his body motionless.

I push my phone toward him, open at the Doe Network picture.

"This guy. This is Tony, right?"

Dad examines the picture and nods. Then I lean over and flick back a few pictures to the initials carved into the workbench leg.

"What about this? Do you know what this is?"

He leans close and Mom props herself up for a clearer view of my phone.

"What is it I'm looking at?" he asks.

"It's a carving that says RIP LM JC 8 26 82." I pause to let this sink in.

"That's the day they went missing," Mom whispers, then translates. "Rest in peace. Luke McLeod. James Cooper. August 26, 1982."

She turns to me. "Where did you find that?"

I stare hard at Mitch's face so I won't miss anything that might flicker there, any clue as to what he knows or is trying to hide. He turns his face down and takes a deep breath.

"In the drive shed, under the workbench," I say.

"Did you tell Zach's father?" he asks and looks up suddenly. His face has changed. He looks his age for the first time ever in my life. He looks tired and worn out, ashen.

"Not yet. Zach's going to tell him though. If he hasn't already. We found it the night we met you there. Is that what you were looking for?"

Mitch shakes his head slowly. "I had no idea it was there."

"Then what were you looking for? Because I know it wasn't your Dodge Charger."

Mitch deflates quickly and his tone softens. "Tony's Mustang. I thought there might still be evidence in it. DNA or something."

Mom hasn't moved for several minutes. She's as still as the wall behind her, a wall that no doubt holds more secrets than it can keep.

Mitch looks at her. "I didn't hurt James. I swear."

"What about Luke?" I ask.

"I didn't hurt anyone. I should have told the police what I knew but I was afraid." He looks at my mother again. "You know what my old man was capable of. I tried to help. It was too late for Luke and Tony. But I tried to help James. I swear I did."

"You saw him that night?" Mom sits up taller. When she speaks, there's barely any sound, it's more like she mouths the words.

"Tony and I were in the basement playing pool. Drinking beer and …" He looks over at me, then at Mom, who nods for him to continue. "We'd been smoking up too. So we weren't in the best frame of mind. Tony thought he heard something outside. He was always paranoid when he got high so I just ignored him. But he insisted he heard someone screaming, so he said he was going to go see what was going on. I really thought he was just hearing things and I had to take a leak so I went upstairs."

He pauses and nobody so much as twitches. I'm not even sure any of us are still breathing.

"The bathroom overlooked the driveway, you know? So I looked out the window while I was there. I could see my dad and his truck in the driveway. And your dad was there too. They had a wheelbarrow. It all happened so fast and it was dark. I don't think I even realized what *was* happening until it was too late. Tony went to the back of the truck and he started screaming at them. He was really upset so I knew it was something bad. I should have run down to calm him, but I froze."

The room fills with silence: my ears pick up the dull hum of the refrigerator, the soft dripping of the kitchen faucet, a raven calling outside the front door.

"They were moving something from the back of the truck into the wheelbarrow. It must have weighed a bit because they both leaned into it. And Tony just wouldn't stop screaming. Dad turned and slugged him in the face. Tony crumpled. He wasn't a huge guy and Dad was strong. I'd seen him drop my mother with one punch to the head like that before. When I was younger. She'd be out for hours."

My phone vibrates and I glance down to see Zach has texted. I pick it up but don't reply. Instead, I lay it face down and turn my attention back to Mitch.

"They barely missed a beat. They stepped over Tony and headed into the forest, down through the cedar trees. Dad was pushing the wheelbarrow and your dad had a rifle. I think. There was enough glow from the porch light to see he was carrying something long under his right arm. And then there was a gunshot later. Maybe from that I just assumed he'd had a gun."

Mom loses her stillness and starts picking at a thread on the sleeve of her shirt. She pulls and twists it around her finger without looking up.

"I didn't know what to do. I was scared. So I went to my bedroom and went to bed. I know it sounds ridiculous but I really didn't know what else to do. I woke up later and Dad ..." He pauses and swallows hard. "He had his rifle, the end of the barrel, pressed up against my head."

Mitch points to his temple and continues.

"He'd never done something like that and I was terrified. He asked me how long I'd been asleep. Somehow I came up with the perfect lie. I told him I'd passed out early. I told him I had a headache and came to bed hours ago. He told me Tony had decided to go home. Then he told me if I was ever asked, I needed to say we'd spent the night together and nobody had left the house. I could barely think with that gun pressing into my skull. So I just lay still."

He glances at Mom, and then away again, as if talking and looking at her is too much data for his brain to process at once. He takes another deep inhale, then rushes through the next part of his story.

"He said if he ever found out I said *anything* about that night to *anyone*, I wouldn't be the only one to suffer. Then he said something about how it was my job to protect you, Sally. Which was best done with silence. After that he left the room. I rolled over and lay in the dark until I heard him go to bed. When I was sure he was asleep I snuck outside to see if I could find Tony. I was pretty sure he wouldn't drive home in the middle of the night but my brain couldn't really process what was going on either. At that point I kept thinking they'd run over the neighbor's dog and had gone off to bury it, that maybe Tony was locked outside or too afraid to come back in. When I got outside, I could hear something banging in the drive shed. I figured it was Tony. But when I opened the door to the workshop, it was James. He said Dad locked him in there and told him to calm down."

Mitch pauses, takes a deep breath as if to refuel.

That's when it hits me and I gasp out loud. Both Mom and Mitch turn to look at me.

"It was James," I say and lean forward in my chair. "It had to be him who carved the initials. Like, it was his goodbye to Luke."

Mitch's expression flickers with recognition but he doesn't stop long to ponder my revelation. He takes another deep breath and lets the momentum carry him forward.

"He was covered in blood — Luke's blood apparently — and he was hysterical. He kept insisting Luke was dead. He said he and Luke had been fishing at the bridge and my dad ran Luke over with his truck. He said he heard them arguing outside the drive shed, your dad and mine. He said my dad was yelling that nobody was going to believe hitting Luke was an accident and there was no way he was going back into custody like when Mom died. And apparently my dad didn't think Tony could keep a secret and insisted he had to be silenced. Nothing made much sense. And James was panicking bad."

Mom continues to play with the thread, Mitch turns his coffee mug in slow circles, and I pick at my cuticles. Nobody makes eye contact.

"Tony's Mustang was in the drive shed, which also didn't make sense to me. I guess Dad put it there to keep it out of sight.

And James was flipping out. I knew I had to get him out of there before Dad woke up. So I put him in Tony's car and took off. I offered to take him home but he was terrified of your father. At least that's what James said. I suggested we go to your Aunt Kathy's but he wasn't listening to reason. He said he had somewhere safe to stay in the city until he figured out what to do next. Or until things settled down. He said something about some cousins in Scarborough."

Mom scowls. "We didn't have cousins in Scarborough."

"I know that now. I realized it a few days later when I asked you about your cousins in Scarborough, suggested maybe James could be with them. You got so angry, told me the only cousins you had lived in Tennessee and you'd never even met them before. I know it sounds ludicrous now, sitting here ..." He gestures around the kitchen. "Sitting here at this same bloody table. But at the time, in all the chaos of that night, it seemed like the only option and I didn't think to doubt him."

I try to imagine what it would have been like to be James that night, so afraid and so alone. My chest tightens into a knot.

"It was late by the time we left our place. Probably two or three in the morning and I knew I didn't have time to get him to the city and get back before Dad woke up. It didn't matter when Dad went to bed, he was always up by dawn. I was so scared. But I dropped James at an all-night coffee shop on the bus route into the city. He said he'd given his wallet to Luke when he waded into the creek to untangle his line and he didn't have any money. So I gave him some cash and my clothes. I thought he'd come back, like in a couple of days. But that was the last time I saw him."

When he finishes speaking, neither Mom nor I say a single word. Mitch stands up and shifts the chair back into place. He tucks it neatly against the edge of the table and holds on to the back of it like it's a child that needs protecting. His head hangs forward, his shoulders slump.

"I'm so sorry. There's not a day that goes by that I'm not sorry."

He steps out of the kitchen and stops to pull on his shoes and coat. Mom doesn't move, just concentrates on the thread. But I follow.

"Where are you going?" I ask, surprised and shocked not only by his confession but that he's apparently going to leave us sitting in the kitchen with the weight of a thirty-five-year-old lie crushing us.

"To the police station. I need to tell them what I just told you. I should have told them back then."

He pushes open the screen door and takes a deep breath.

"Mitch!" Mom calls out from the kitchen.

He pauses and waits to hear what she has to say.

"What happened to his clothes?"

"I hid them under a floorboard in the back of the drive shed. Inside an old tire tube. That's why I really came back. I was pretty sure the Mustang was long gone but the clothes I knew I could turn in as evidence. I thought I could do the right thing. For a change."

ZACH 12

Dad normally gives off an air of confidence, maybe even a bit of tough guy. I mean, to the rest of the world, right? To me, now, he's just a dad. But when I was little, like five or six, he was my hero. I can't imagine any little kid not being in awe of a parent who is a police officer. But today, I'm seeing a new side of him. I'm seeing the fumbling, muttering, grumpy version of my normally controlled father. I guess I shouldn't be too surprised, or judgmental. It's not like he does press conferences all the time — there's not much crime in Clarendon to report. But today, in less than an hour, he has to go down to the police station to deliver a speech to the media. And to make matters worse, there's going to be local and national coverage, and maybe even an international news outlet or two. Apparently, decades-old cold cases draw a lot of attention once they're solved.

He's standing at the bathroom mirror, fighting with his police-issued navy blue tie. He looks good in his uniform: broad, official, tidy. If he has a chance of winning over Sally, today would be the day. I wonder if that's part of the problem.

"You want a hand with that?" I ask from the bathroom door as I watch him untie it and line up the ends again.

"Like you know how to tie a tie," he snaps. He glances over at me and scowls when he sees my perfectly tied double Windsor knot.

"YouTube," I offer. "Here, give it to me."

He rips off the tie and hands it over. I shuffle into the bathroom and take up the space in front of the mirror so that he has to step over by the shower. Then I wrap the tie around my neck, tie the knot, loosen it, and hand it back to him. I don't bother with instructions. Even I know when to fly under the radar.

He mutters, "Thanks," then checks his hair in the mirror.

"You look great," I say, hoping to calm his nerves. "You're going to do great too."

His lips tighten into a thin line and he turns to give me the once-over. "You look pretty good yourself."

I follow Dad down the stairs to the kitchen and watch him straighten the junk mail into equal piles, then take last night's pots from the drying rack to stack in the cupboard. I can feel the nervous energy spilling onto the floor around him.

"Hey, Dad," I say to break the trance of his feverish movement. "Don't you have to leave, like, now?"

He stops with a pot in his hand, glances at the clock on the stove, and sighs. "These will have to wait," he says bitterly, as if his day is ruined now that the kitchen counter isn't as tidy as the junk mail.

I step forward and take the pot from him. "I'll take care of these. You should get going."

"I'll see you there?" he asks as he pulls on his blazer and leans down to tie his shoes.

"Sally and Kate are picking me up at half past," I say as I follow him into the mudroom and open the door. He nods absently and strides past me to the police cruiser.

"Good luck," I shout as he opens the car door. He doesn't reply but I don't mind. After all, it's not every day he gets to let the world know his team closed two cold cases in the same week.

When Dad leaves, I throw the remaining dishes into cupboards, grab my jacket, and wait by the door. I'm partway outside before Sally puts the car into park. I can't risk being late.

"You clean up good," Sally says when I climb into the back seat.

"You too," I say, mostly to Kate, who's wearing a swishy floral skirt with her black Blundstones and a biker-style jacket. It sounds like a strange combination but somehow it works for her.

Sally glances at me in the rearview mirror and I know she's onto me. I flash an exaggerated smile.

"Your dad must be pretty excited," she says.

"Dad? He doesn't get too nervous about these sorts of things," I lie, more for my benefit than his.

Kate turns halfway in her seat and looks me up and down. I know she's dying to make some quip about the tie and blazer, but she smiles instead.

"We were at the restaurant this morning and the town was crawling with press vans. The CBC film crew was taking footage of the town hall and the CTV crew was at the park in front of that memorial bench. This is a big deal." She pauses, then adds quietly, "And we won't get any credit whatsoever."

Sally scowls and speaks somberly. "The important thing is not who solved what, but that two families will finally have some closure after thirty-five years."

Her words take us all by surprise, even her, and the car floods with silence faster than the spring runoff fills the ditches along Valley Road in March. Nobody will say his name, but we're all thinking about James. Kate sighs and looks out the window. I check my phone. Sally grips the steering wheel and stares dead ahead.

We park behind the station in the space labeled Detective Whitchurch and find a place to stand in a roped-off section to the side of the podium where Dad will be making his statement to the press. It's a reserved area for families and friends of the police force. The area in front of the podium is standing room only with reporters and camera crews jostling for position. Dad isn't outside yet but still has ten minutes until go time. I imagine him pacing in his office, muttering and wringing hands, while trying to appear calm and collected.

Out beyond the press area, I can see people I know: friends, parents of friends, teachers, acquaintances from school and sports teams, like from back when I still played in the Little Leagues. As I scan the crowd, I see Josh standing on the far side of the parking lot on a small hill, waving like a maniac. I smile and shake my head when he shoots me the thumbs-up, knowing that even if nobody else has noticed, at least he sees me standing shoulder to shoulder with the girl he told me only a few weeks ago was completely out of my league. If I wasn't happier, I'd flip him the bird.

"Where's your dad?" I lean over and whisper into Kate's hair, pausing long enough to inhale her vanilla-scented conditioner and then a bit longer in case anyone from school, besides Josh, is watching.

She pulls out her phone, flicks through a couple of screens, blasts off a quick text, films the crowd, then shoves it back in her jacket pocket.

"I dunno. I haven't heard from him today. I texted him about the press conference though, so he wouldn't miss it."

Finally, Dad steps out a side door of the police station, flanked by two officers I've known my whole life. They walk stiffly to the podium and squint out at the crowd. Cameras flash like the paparazzi for movie stars on the red carpet at the Oscars. But Dad is standing on plain old black pavement, with only the yellow-brick police station as a backdrop.

He taps the microphone and clears his throat, stares straight ahead and flattens his speaking notes on the top of the podium. I feel Kate's hand in mine suddenly, and when I glance down, I see she's holding her mother's hand too so that we three are joined like old-fashioned paper dolls.

I glance over and note that Sally looks pale. I reach into the front pocket of my dress pants with my free hand and offer her a Tums. I've been suffering a bit of acid reflux lately. Call it nerves. Or anxiety. Or love.

Sally tilts her head like she's trying to figure something out, but finally takes a Tums and pops it into her mouth. "Thanks," she mouths.

I lean my face close to Kate again. "Did you post about the press conference on Facebook?"

She nods. "On Instagram too."

Then Dad begins to speak and a hush falls over the crowd. It's so still and quiet suddenly, it feels like a funeral. Even the clouds overhead seem to stop moving, the birds are suddenly quiet, there isn't even a hint of traffic on the surrounding streets.

"Good afternoon. My name is Detective Whitchurch. I want to start by thanking members of the press for coming today on such short notice."

He pauses and clears his throat, looks out across the crowd, and flattens his speaking notes again. And then again. I worry he's going to tear the paper if he keeps smoothing it.

"Today I want to update you on two cold cases. Both of which date back to 1982. Thanks to tips received from members of the public, we have had significant breaks in both cases that I want to share with you."

Kate and I squeeze our hands at the same time when he mentions "tips received from members of the public."

"The remains of two males were found on a property on the second concession outside of Clarendon. Forensic reports have determined that one of the individuals died as a result of severe trauma to the chest. The other died as a result of a gunshot wound. DNA testing has confirmed the identity of the first individual as Luke Eric McLeod."

At the mention of Luke's name someone in the crowd begins to cry and I look to see who it is. But everyone else also turns and starts to look around so it's impossible to tell.

Dad continues. "The second set of remains has been confirmed as belonging to Anthony Frank Lomangino."

At this point the press area erupts into chaos. Reporters begin shouting questions, lobbing them at Dad faster than he can blink back the camera flashes. Camera crews shove fuzzy microphones on long poles at the podium, like an army of lances aimed at the same target.

"Where on the property were the remains found?"

"Why didn't the police search that property before now?"

"What led you to the remains?"

"What's the connection between Luke and Anthony?"

"Is there any evidence that Luke and Anthony were acquainted?"

"Did you find any clues about the whereabouts of James Cooper?"

Dad raises his hands to settle the crowd, and when the uproar quiets, he resumes his speech.

"The police currently have an adult male in custody. Peter Goheen is cooperating with law enforcement officials and has made a full statement to the police. His version of events has been substantiated by a key witness and evidence found at and around the scene of the crime."

Dad takes a big breath and grips the edges of the podium as if he's afraid of floating away, or maybe being toppled by the gravity of what he is about to say. He doesn't pause long before he speaks again.

"Mr. Goheen is being charged with second-degree murder in the death of Luke Eric McLeod and with first-degree murder in the death of Anthony Frank Lomangino. He's also being charged with concealment of a homicidal death and obstruction of justice. The investigation continues and at this time we have no further information to share. Thank you."

Dad steps back from the microphone and the volley of questions begin again.

"What made Peter Goheen testify suddenly?"

"Does this have anything to do with his son, who was seen in the area recently?"

"Is Mitch Goheen the key witness? Why didn't he come forward before now?"

"What about James?" a tall, male reporter shouts above the racket. "What happened to James Cooper?"

I glance over at Sally. Her free hand is tucked behind her neck and she's trembling. But she straightens her shoulders and takes a deep breath. "That's the goddamned million-dollar question, isn't it?" she mutters.

When the press conference finishes, the crowd breaks up slowly. The news reporters and camera crews pack up their gear and are the first to leave. Some locals move down the street, back toward their houses, but others stand in the parking lot talking in clusters, recounting what my father said, and speculating about Peter and Mitch Goheen and, of course, about James.

I see Dad talking to an elderly man with a walker who is flanked by a man and a woman I don't recognize. Dad sees me looking in his direction and motions for me to join them, so I walk over slowly. There's something about their huddle that calls for caution, solemnity. When I get close enough, Dad puts his hand on my shoulder. It's a gesture of ownership, but also of pride, and I swell a little.

"Zach, I'd like you to meet John McLeod, his daughter, Natalie, and his son, Ben."

The realization that I'm staring at Luke McLeod's family slams into me hard and I feel winded. But I try not to let on and gulp back a lungful of air. I hold out my hand in greeting. Ben takes the offer first. He has a firm grip, and when I look into his face, I see so much kindness I feel a lump form in the back of my throat.

"Your dad told us you live in our old house," Ben says.

I nod and swallow hard.

"I didn't know until recently. But yes. We do."

Ben recedes when Natalie reaches out to shake my hand.

"It's very nice to meet you, Zach. Apparently, you have Luke's old bedroom."

Suddenly the world shifts. My perspective widens and stretches. I understand when I hear her words that they are looking at a kid the same age as their brother the last time they saw him, the kid who now sleeps in the same room.

Finally, Mr. McLeod stretches out his right hand. He doesn't reach very far and he grips the walker tightly with his left hand at the same time. I have to step forward to make the connection.

"Your father tells us you helped uncover some key evidence. We're very grateful."

I glance at Dad quickly, surprised to have been given any credit at all. Then I train my eyes back on Mr. McLeod.

"It wasn't on purpose. And it wasn't just me," I stammer. His grip on my hand loosens and he puts both hands on the walker again. "My friend, Kate, she helped a lot. Kate Cooper. I mean, if it wasn't for her …"

"We'll be sure to thank her too. But we want you to know how much this closure means to us," he says.

Ben and Natalie nod in agreement and Natalie puts her hand on her father's arm. It's a protective movement.

"I'm sorry," I stammer again and my eyes flicker across Ben and Natalie's faces. "I'm sorry about your brother."

Now it's Natalie's turn to swallow hard. Her face starts to crumple but she reaches down deep, into some invisible reservoir, and finds her composure again. She smiles graciously but the nostalgia has been replaced by something new, perhaps a desire for the day to be over.

Dad puts his hand back on my shoulder and I immediately recognize the signal that it's time for me to go. I melt into the crowd and watch Sally and Kate take their turn with the McLeods.

By the time everyone has left the press conference, it looks as if the fall fair was in town. The grounds of the police station are strewn with empty drink bottles and strands of yellow police tape. One of Dad's colleagues hands us garbage bags and Kate and I start to pick up the trash while Sally and Dad stand by the podium talking.

"Anything on Facebook?" I ask.

Kate drops her garbage bag and checks her phone. She shakes her head. "Nope. But that doesn't mean he didn't see my posts." She puts her phone in her back pocket and continues to fill her bag.

When the grounds are clean, we drag our bags of garbage over to where Dad and Sally are talking and drop them at Dad's feet.

"This is everything," I say.

He looks up, surprised, and maybe a bit annoyed to be interrupted. "Thanks for helping out," he says. "That's terrific. Now, if you tie those off and put them in the dumpster out back, I'll owe you dinner and a movie."

Kate raises her eyebrows and shoots me a look of skepticism. I shrug. Sometimes there's no figuring out my father. But he's clearly in a good mood and I'm not going to complain. Maybe he's relieved the whole press conference is over. Maybe seeing the McLeods gave him some kind of boost. Maybe he's having a good conversation with Sally.

We're halfway to the dumpster when Dad calls out, "By the way, when you're done there, I'd like if the four of us could go inside and talk. Maybe in my office?"

Kate and I share another look. It's obvious something is up.

× × ×

Dad's office looks and smells exactly the same as it always does. Like déjà vu. Kate, Sally, and I take seats across from him and he sits behind his desk.

"I think that went as well as can be expected," he says and leans back in his chair.

"There was a good turnout," Sally agrees.

"And you didn't sound like a moron," I offer.

Dad shoots me a warning look and Kate kicks at my foot playfully.

"It was nice to see the McLeods," Sally says.

Dad's lips form a straight line, a grimace. He loosens his tie and sighs.

"It was," he says. "I'm just sorry Mrs. McLeod didn't live long enough to find out what happened to her son."

It's a sobering thought and I get lost in imagining how the family distracted themselves day to day, how Dad would distract himself if he was in the same situation. How Mom might. I skip back to Dad and imagine him sitting in the dusty dining room with boxes of cold case notes stacked up around him on the table, empty soup and pop cans littered on the floor by his feet. But my daydream is interrupted.

"I wanted to let you know Peter Goheen made a full confession about his role in the deaths of both boys."

Sally sucks in her breath.

"If it wasn't for Mitch, we wouldn't have been able to accomplish this so quickly. Maybe not at all. He led us to some critical evidence. I think you know what I'm talking about. Anyhow, without his help we wouldn't have the slam dunk we do. With what Mitch was able to give us, well, it was enough to convince Peter Goheen to cooperate finally, or that not cooperating was futile."

I sneak a glance at Kate and she's smiling. For the first time in days she seems relaxed and I wonder if she's changed her mind about Hicksville yet.

Dad continues. "In exchange for his testimony, and for cooperating with the police, Mitch has been granted immunity from any repercussions regarding the false information he provided in his previous testimony in 1982."

Kate sits up straight. "So where is he?"

Sally takes Kate's hand and holds it like it's made of glass. "I'm sorry, sweetie. He went back to Australia. He left last night."

Kate slouches in her chair. She extends her legs straight out in front of her and lowers her chin.

"He's terrible with goodbyes. You know that. And he didn't want to stay for the press conference. You know how people talk. He'd have been hounded. But he has to come back for the trial in a few months. And he's going to call when he gets home. You can talk to him then."

Dad clears his throat.

"Sally, Peter Goheen said something curious that I thought you should know."

Sally glances up but says nothing, waiting for Dad to continue.

"He said your dad always blamed him. Suspected him of killing James even though he swore up and down he didn't lay a finger on the boy. That the kid just disappeared into thin air."

Sally doesn't respond. It's like she doesn't have the mental energy to crack open her reserve of hope again.

Sally and Kate seem consumed by their private thoughts and Dad turns his attention to the open laptop on his desk. I watch them in turn and think about how much has changed in only a few weeks. It seems unimaginable that I haven't known Kate my whole life. She seems so central, so consuming, so essential. The tight pressure in my chest lets go. I think about how I've only had one full-on panic attack since summer, that I helped solve two cold cases, that the coolest girl in school is my best friend, maybe even my girlfriend. Long strands of my hair tickle my cheek and I wipe them back off my face. Then I make a promise to myself. Tomorrow I'm going to get myself to a barber. I won't tell Kate, but I smile to myself when I imagine her reaction to seeing me for the first time with an actual haircut. She deserves the best version of me.

EPILOGUE

When the front door swings open, I feel a small rush of anxiety. The restaurant closes in half an hour and the three tables are finishing their dessert specials: homemade turmeric latte gelato and cinnamon wafers. I'm relieved to see that the man who walked in is alone. If he doesn't linger, Mom and I might get home by nine. It's been a long first week at the restaurant and I'm feeling a little beat up. First there was the press conference, then the grand opening, and every night since the restaurant has been jammed. Tonight is no different. We've already served twenty-six dinners, which is a lot for just me and Mom to handle, even with a limited menu. Then, of course, there's schoolwork. And Zach.

The man is tall, slender, dressed in jeans and a black jacket. His hair is cut short and when he sits down I notice a thin spot at the crown of his head. He's taken a seat by the front window, away from the other customers, and settled in with his back to the wall and a view of the entire restaurant.

"Can I bring you something to drink?" I ask when I hand him the menu on a narrow wooden clipboard.

"Just a soda," he says, smiling.

"A soda?"

"A Coke? Or Pepsi?"

"We have San Pellegrino," I suggest. "Orange, pomegranate, or lemon. They're carbonated."

"Lemon, thanks," he says and glances down at the menu.

"I'll be right back if you have any questions about the menu, and to tell you about our Grand Opening Special," I say, then head over to the cash register to ring out the elderly couple who stretched their meal over an hour but suddenly seem in a rush to leave.

"How was everything?" I ask as I ring them up.

"Just lovely. Nice to have a five-star meal in Clarendon for a change," the gentleman says. He pulls a gray tweed hat over his thinning hair, then hands me his credit card.

"You tell your mother the pumpkin gnocchi was fantastic," the lady says as she pockets a couple of mints from the wooden bowl by the cash register. "And tell her Mrs. Amberley says hello. She'll know who I am."

I smile and complete the transaction, then head back to the single man's table with a tall glass of ice and a can of lemon-flavored San Pellegrino.

"Do you have any questions about the menu?"

The man shakes his head and hands back the clipboard.

"Have you decided what you'd like to order?"

I use my friendliest voice and smile generously, the way Mom coached.

"I have. I'd like the garam masala chicken stew with dumplings. Not too sure about the garam masala part but I can't pass up chicken and dumplings." He cracks open his San Pellegrino and pours some into the glass. "Oh, and can I have the pear salad to start?"

"Great choice," I say and turn around as he takes the first sip of his drink.

When the next table is finished, I give them their bill and cash them out. They leave with promises to come back again and satisfied smiles on their faces. My phone vibrates in my back pocket and I sneak it out to take a look. It's a text from Zach.

Busy there tonight?

Uggggg

Gonna get out on time?

Hope so. Late customer. But just a single guy.

Date stood him up?

I dunno.

See you later?

Definitely. I'll text when we leave.

Mom rings the bell and I startle, almost dropping my phone. But I recover and return it to my back pocket. Then I push through the kitchen door, grab the salad plate, and deliver it with a bundle of cutlery to the man at the window table.

"This place is new?" he asks, but in a way that doesn't expect an answer. He looks around the small dining room and I follow his gaze. It's nothing short of a miracle to see what Mom has pulled off so quickly.

"Yep, we just opened this week."

"Business has been good?"

"So far, yes. It's always a risk opening a restaurant in a small town, I guess. But my mom knows what she's doing."

"Your mom is *Sally*?"

"The one and only," I say flippantly. "She doesn't know a thing about horses or cars, but she definitely knows her way around a kitchen."

The man spears a sliver of Asiago and a slice of shaved pear and puts it in his mouth, then nods approvingly. I see him line up his second bite out of the corner of my eye as I walk away.

When the table of four leaves, I clear their dishes and put clean linens on all of the tables so they'll be ready to go tomorrow night.

"Looks like I'm the last customer of the night," the man observes as I bring him his bowl of chicken and dumplings.

"Take your time. There's no rush," I say, before turning off the OPEN sign.

The street is almost empty and the sky has turned a deep gray. Other than our restaurant and the variety store across the street, all the other buildings along the main street are dark.

"These dumplings are outstanding," the man offers.

"I'm glad you like them. My mom adapted her mother's recipe. Apparently a favorite at Clarendon potlucks for decades."

He swallows, then wipes his mouth with the cloth napkin. "The flavoring, it's a nice touch. I didn't think anyone could improve on chicken and dumplings, but I was wrong. Tell your mom it's nice to see the classics on a menu these days. Everyone needs comfort food now and then."

"Your mom used to make them too?"

"Every Sunday night. Dumplings and Disney."

I laugh. "My mom used to watch that show too. She said there wasn't anything else to do in a small town on Sundays but watch whatever was on TV."

"That's the truth."

"You're from a small town?"

"I grew up in a small town." He pauses and looks out the

window at the darkening street. "But I live in a city now. Knox-ville. It's in Tennessee."

I'm standing at the counter wrapping cutlery in cloth napkins and can hear Mom in the kitchen putting things away, cleaning up for the night.

"You're a long way from home."

"I travel a lot for work. It's hard sometimes. I miss my family."

My instinct is to ask what sort of business would bring anyone to Clarendon. But I go for a tip-getting question instead.

"Do you have a big family in Tennessee?"

He waits a bit too long to reply, chews his chicken, then swirls the last piece of dumpling in the puddle of gravy.

"Not too big. My parents have both passed away. I haven't seen my sister in years. But I'm married and we have two sons, about your age. And some extended family."

"Maybe you should reach out to your sister? She probably misses you," I say, thinking about how much Mom misses James.

"I dunno. Life's funny. It's not always easy to pick up where you left off."

He drinks the last of his San Pellegrino, taps the can with the fingernail of his index finger, smiles across the room at me. He has a nice smile, friendly, easygoing.

I take his plate and cutlery. "Coffee? Dessert? The gelato is amazing."

"Sure. I'll give the gelato a try. And a coffee too please. I have some driving to do after this."

When I drop off his coffee and dessert, he smiles warmly at me, and even though I normally hate making small talk with strangers, this man makes me feel comfortable.

"So what's it like living here?"

I continue to wipe down the salt and pepper shakers while I talk. "Actually, I don't really know. We just moved here from the west coast."

"That must have been a big adjustment. How long has it been?"

"It's definitely been a big adjustment," I say. "How long? Let me see. We moved at the beginning of September. So almost six weeks." I do the calculation in my mind, surprised to realize that somewhere along the way I'd stopped counting. "Forty days to be exact!"

"How do you like it so far?"

"Well. I hated it at first." I smile wryly. "But now it's growing on me, I guess."

The door to the kitchen swings open and Mom's head appears. I do a bit of a double take. She never looks like my mom when she's in her chef clothes with her hair tucked under a black cap. She's checking to see who's left in the dining room and if I've turned off the OPEN sign.

The man looks up and smiles. "That was the best meal I've had in ages. My compliments to the chef."

He raises his coffee cup.

"Thanks. I'm glad you enjoyed it." Mom beams. "I hope you'll come again. I'll be changing up the menu every month with weekly specials."

She disappears into the kitchen and the man rummages in his back pocket for his wallet. I watch from where I'm stacking clean glasses behind the counter.

"Do you need the machine?"

"I'm doing it old school," he says, fishing out some bills.

He stands up and lays money on the table, then weighs it down with his coffee cup.

"Can I bring you some change?"

"That's okay. It's all good. Thanks for a great meal. And great service too."

He moves toward the door, pauses, and looks around as if he's forgotten something.

"Thanks again. Come back soon. Like, if you're in the area for business again," I say.

He nods, waves, and slips outside onto the dark street. When I lock the door behind him, I see the outline of his slender shape walking away down the sidewalk.

"Last customer's gone," I shout out to Mom. "I locked the door and turned off the front lights."

I stop at the table to pick up the last dishes of the night. That's when I realize the man left a hundred-dollar bill for a thirty-nine-dollar meal.

"Whoah," I call out. "Nice tipper!"

I pocket the bill, then notice a worn photograph lying face up on the table. I pick it up to examine closer. It's a picture of the man, a few years younger and with more hair, surrounded by people who I assume are his family: two young boys, a woman with her arm around him, other adults and a few teenagers, and a much older lady — does she look familiar? I lean close to the window and look in both directions, in case the man is still within sight and I can return the photo. But the sidewalk is empty.

I turn over the photo and read a line of handwriting: *Not all that is lost is ready to be found. Be patient.*

"What's that?" Mom asks. She's standing behind me.

"An old photograph. That man left it with a huge tip."

"He left you a photograph?" she asks and pinches her eyebrows into a question mark in the middle.

"He must have left it by accident," I suggest.

"Let me see," she says.

I hand Mom the photo, then pick up the coffee cup and gelato bowl. Mom is staring intently at the picture in her hand. Something about the expression on her face turns the blood in my veins to ice and a shiver rattles the length of my spine. My knees feel weak.

"What's wrong?"

Mom points to the older lady in the photo. "That's Grandma." She rushes to the front door, unlocks it, and steps through in one fluid motion. She looks both ways up the street, the overhead streetlight casting her in an orange glow.

"What's wrong?" I ask again, this time from where I'm standing beside her on the sidewalk.

"I think that was ... James? Maybe?" she whispers. "I don't know ... How ..." The color drains from her face and she walks back inside to search the table where he was sitting.

"What are you looking for?" I ask.

"I don't know? Anything else he might have left behind."

"He left a big tip," I offer, then pull the hundred-dollar bill out of my pocket and examine it closely. That's when I notice something I didn't before. In the second zero there are a series of letters written in pencil: *XOX CJG.*

I look up at Mom and smile so wide I think my face is going to burst open.

"What?" Mom takes the bill to see what I'm looking at. "What's that?"

"He's been watching!" I shriek. "On Facebook!"

Mom sits down slowly in his chair, the photograph gripped tightly in her hand. "I don't understand."

"I'll show you," I say and pull out my phone to school my mother on the power of social media, starting with the Facebook page *What's Happening in Clarendon*.

I scroll to my post about the grand opening of Mustang Sally's and show Mom the string of comments. Strangers have posted about how great it is to have a new restaurant in town and old classmates of my mother's have welcomed her back to the community, promising to come in for dinner soon. About forty comments in, there's one from CJ Grover: *Can't wait for a taste of home.*

I'm so excited my voice trembles. "See. That's him. He signed the same initials on the bill." I pull out the bill to show her, my hands shaking with excitement.

I flip over to his personal page and show Mom his profile picture, a new one he posted a few hours ago. She takes my phone and pulls the screen close to her face.

"I can see it!" she whispers, then looks up at me with a light so intense in her eyes I would have to look away if she wasn't my mother. "His mouth is the same. And the eyes. That mischief is still in them."

Can you imagine seeing a picture of your *presumed dead* brother after thirty-five years? That's the look on Mom's face. It's this weird mix of wonder and disbelief, and layered over that there's so much love and gratitude I can feel it pouring out of her and seeping into me.

I show her how to scroll through his posts and photos and she sits there, mesmerized, laughing at stupid memes and zooming in on photos of his sons.

"This older one. He really looks like James at that age. The same golden hair. What a cutie."

"Mom?" I say finally and she looks up as if she's surprised to see me standing there. "We should go home. You can see the pictures much better on a laptop."

That's what I say, but really I'm thinking about Zach coming over before bedtime and our window of opportunity is closing. I can't wait to tell him about James showing up. That I met my actual *presumed dead* uncle.

Mom stands up and hands me the phone. She glances at her watch and shakes her head at the time.

"It's so late. Yes, let's get you home!" she says.

I text Zach: *On our way.*

The drive home is quiet. I sit in the dark car and wonder about James appearing suddenly like that. What must it have been like for him to step back into his past? I wonder if he's sneaked back other times and how long he's been keeping an eye on Clarendon.

Not all that is lost is ready to be found. Be patient.

"Do you think he came back because your dad's dead finally and Peter Goheen's in custody? I mean, no offense on the dead dad thing," I say in a musing sort of way.

Mom doesn't speak right away. She stares ahead at the dark road and grips the steering wheel, but the worry lines on her face seem suddenly diminished.

"I'm sure he had ... *has* ... a lot of reasons for staying away. Certainly Dad and Mr. Goheen played a big role. I mean Mitch and I stayed away too for many, many years. We'd have done anything to be safe from their reach. But then there was also Luke and Tony. Maybe he felt responsible somehow. Maybe he couldn't face the McLeods, knowing Luke was dead and he wasn't."

There's so much to process, I have a hard time knowing what thoughts to pursue first. My head is like a bowl of spaghetti noodles, all tangled up and impossible to separate into single strands.

"But do you think it's strange he never made contact with you all that time? I mean, you were close, right?"

Mom shrugs but doesn't take her hands off the steering wheel or her eyes off the road. Her face is lit up from the lights on the dashboard, making her appear so much younger I can almost feel her seventeen-year-old self shining through the decades.

"We were young. And the night he left, it would have been so terrifying. Can you imagine watching your friend dying? Your own father helping to cover it up? So I don't know. Maybe Mom didn't want us to be in touch. Maybe she thought we'd all be safer if I didn't know the truth. Maybe he just moved on with his life."

What she says makes sense, so I nod to myself. I sit still, hunt down thoughts and explanations, try to make sense of every-thing I've learned in the past forty days. Mom clears her throat and continues.

"Maybe he wants the trial to be over and the interest in the case to die down before he makes a grand entrance. Or maybe he never will. Whatever his reasoning, I'm sure it's valid. But just knowing he's *alive* …" Her voice catches and she swallows hard, lifts one hand off the steering wheel, and wipes it along the bottom of her eyelids. Then she sighs so deep and long, I had no idea there was that much room in her lungs.

When we get home, Mom doesn't even take off her shoes before she sets herself down at the kitchen table with her laptop.

I open up the browser to James's page on Facebook but she shakes her head.

"Can you open up that other page. The one about Clarendon?"

I navigate to the *What's Happening in Clarendon* page and she scrolls through the comments again.

"Do you want to send him a message?"

"Like an email?" she asks.

"I was thinking of something less direct. Just to let him know *you know* it's him, but without scaring him off. I mean, he said to be patient, right? We should respect his privacy."

I turn the laptop toward me and make a new post on the page.

My mother, Sally Cooper, and I want to thank everyone for making the Grand Opening of Mustang Sally's a huge success! Thank you to new friends and old friends for coming by and trying our homemade classics with a twist. We cherish connecting and reconnecting. Come back soon!

The laptop dings almost immediately.

"What was that?" my mother asks.

"He just responded to your post. With a heart emoji."

Mom smiles so wide I think her face might crack open like a Christmas walnut. She finds her way back to his page and starts scrolling through his posts again. It isn't long before she's lost in another world, a world she thought was forever gone.

I hear Zach knock on the door and I slip from the kitchen.

"Hey," he says when I open the door. He's wearing a lined jean jacket and his hands are tucked deep in his pockets. The nights are definitely turning cold and the last few mornings I've left tracks in the frost when I walked across the grass to the school bus.

"Hey," I say and invite him inside.

He kicks off his shoes and we pad in our socked feet down the hall to the living room, moving soundlessly past the kitchen. He glances in and sees Mom on the laptop, but she hasn't registered that anyone else is in the house.

Zach and I sit together on the same end of the couch and I turn on the TV.

"So you'll never guess who came by the restaurant tonight," I say casually, even though I'm bursting to tell him.

"Who?"

"Guess!"

"You said I'll never guess," he says sarcastically and smiles, "so just tell me."

"James!"

He turns to face me, his eyes squinting in confusion.

"*James Cooper*, James?"

I nod enthusiastically and pull out the hundred-dollar bill to show him the initials. He takes it and turns it over and over as if there might be another clue left to be discovered.

"Mom's on Facebook right now. He responded to a post I made."

"Did they talk?" Zach asks, still trying to wrap his mind around this bizarre turn of events.

"No. He left a note saying he wasn't ready yet and to be patient."

"So he's alive? He's actually really alive?"

I nod. "Can you believe it?"

We sit for a moment in the quiet and listen to Mom a room away in the kitchen, laughing at something she's seen on James's Facebook feed.

Zach is the first to break the silence. "So how's your new video project coming along?"

One of the things I like best about Zach is that he's interested in me and that he listens when I talk. He remembers what I've said and asks about what I'm doing even when we aren't together. Austin was never like that. He spent more time talking about himself or complaining about how his father never listened to him.

"Good," I say brightly. "Only a couple more hours of editing. It's going to run probably thirty minutes when it's done and I've got some great shots. I can't wait for you to see it."

"You don't think I'll be insulted? I mean, aren't you sort of mocking my hometown?"

He picks up my hand and plays with my fingers absently before he entwines his into mine and it feels like our hands are one unit.

"You have to give it a chance. I think you'll see that I portray my time here pretty fairly, and besides, I've got some amazing footage of some really compelling moments."

"Do you think your YouTube subscribers will stick with you?"

I shrug, and to be honest, I don't care that much anymore.

"Did you come up with a title?"

I can't help but smirk because I'd just thought of the perfect title on our way home from the restaurant. And I love it! Maybe even more than the video. When I'm finished, I'm sure it's going to be good enough for a film school submission.

"Forty Days in Hicksville," I say, then add quickly, "Don't roll your eyes! There's a character arc. It shows how my point of view changes over time."

Zach shakes his head in mock defeat and leans toward me. He stretches his arm out as if to embrace me, and before I realize he's reaching for the remote, I kiss him. On the lips.

He lingers, then pulls his face back slightly.

"That was so much better than what I was going to do," he says softly, and kisses me again, dissolving any embarrassment I might have felt had he let the mix-up hang between us.

It's our first kiss. Soft. Tender. Electric. I want to melt into him and stay there. Warm and happy. Perfect.

✖ ✖ ✖

When Zach leaves for the night, I close the door behind him reluctantly. I want to rush onto the porch for one more kiss, but I know that will lead to another and another, and we've already spent the past forty minutes trying to say goodbye as it is. A flutter in my chest takes me by surprise and I lean back against the doorframe to steady myself. I see Mom is still on the laptop in the kitchen when I finally feel ready to try walking again. Her face is inclined toward the screen and radiates so much joy it hurts to watch because I know how much pain came before. I don't interrupt to say good night, but before I turn away, I glance around the room. There are dishes in the drying rack from lunch and a stack of opened mail on the windowsill. My sweater is draped over one of the chairs and the garbage can needs emptying. The walls are still painted a shade of green that was last popular in the 1980s, but it's not such a bad color, I realize now, kind of cool in a retro kind of way. It's a good house, I think to myself. Sure, it's outdated and it smelled weird when we first arrived, but for the first time it doesn't feel like it's filled with dark secrets and ghosts.

It feels like hope and optimism.

It feels like home.

ACKNOWLEDGMENTS

As it turns out, writing is a team sport and it took a lot of people to get this book across the finish line. Thanks to everyone who cheered from the sidelines and those who suggested new strategies at time-out. In particular, I want to thank John Denison for early inspiration; Bella Goudie and Katona Files for being beta readers; the amazing Stacey Kondla for getting me back on the field when I threatened to give up; everyone at The Rights Factory who ended up reading some version of this book at some point (there were quite a few of you!); Barry Jowett for his brilliant, insightful editing; and the entire team at Cormorant Books for taking a chance on me and *40 Days in Hicksville*. And last, but of course not least, thank you to everyone who has ever read one of my books and to everyone who reads this one. Without readers, there would be no books.

CHRISTINA KILBOURNE is an award-winning author of adult, young adult, and middle-grade fiction. Her books have won the Manitoba Young Readers Choice Award, a Snow Willow Award, and a Red Cedar Award and have been nominated for numerous others. She was born in Southwestern Ontario but spent her school years in Muskoka where she attended a two-room country school. In her spare time, Kilbourne enjoys travelling, skiing, hiking, kayaking, and anything else that keeps her moving. She lives in Bracebridge, Ontario.